THE KEY TO VIOLET ROSE

LORI LAIRD

FOR MY HILLBILLY...

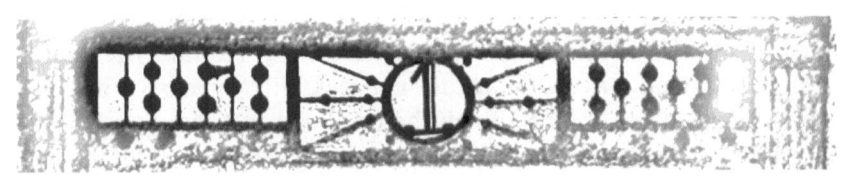

Her high heels sank into the faded turquoise carpet with each step. Careful not to twist an ankle, Sunny wondered why they would put so much padding on the floor in the first place. The entire building had an offensively overwhelming floral aroma. Speaking in hushed tones, the guests looked at photo collages and flower arrangements as they slowly filed in. It seemed the whole town had shown up, but there was no need for Sunny to wait in line. In the main room, wooden folding chairs were positioned in uniform rows facing the guest of honor, while cushioned armchairs and sofas with tacky upholstery lined the walls. She noticed a dimly lit sitting room off to the side and hoped there was an outlet where she could charge her phone. First, she would have to make her way through the crowd surrounding the man of the hour to make her presence known. She knew she'd never hear the end of it otherwise.

The first glimpse she got of him was in between an old couple walking across the overly cushioned floor with what she could only assume were matching his-and-her canes. She thought she recognized them from her grandmother's church, but she couldn't be sure. The last time she had gone to a Sunday sermon was nearly twenty years ago when she was still a child. Once the cane-wielding couple had cleared out, she was able to really see him. Mr. Howard Richmond, her grandfather, was stuffed in an unnecessarily expensive box. He looked odd to her, which she attributed to the fact that he was now dead. The last time she'd seen him he was full of life, cracking jokes, and being the grandfather she knew and loved. Before she had a chance to go up to him she heard the one voice she had been anticipating.

"My baby! Everyone get out of my way so I can hug my baby girl!" Sunny's mother, Willow, had been surrounded by three elderly couples who had been friends of Howard's.

"Hey, mom," Sunny said through a sympathetic smile.

"Oh, I'm so happy to see my sweet Sunny." Willow hugged her daughter, and whispered in her ear, "*Try and act like a normal person instead of a robot, okay? Maybe shed a tear at daddy's casket or somethin'.*" She kissed her on the cheek and stepped back to the group of mourners with whom she had been speaking.

Sunny knew exactly what her mother was talking about, because showing her emotions was not something she excelled at. She approached her grandfather's casket and stood silently in front of him. She wasn't sure what she was supposed to do at this point. Was she supposed to talk to him? Pray to someone or something? Should she do as her mother suggested and cry? She didn't do any of those things. Instead she stood awkwardly for thirty seconds and then went in search of an outlet to charge her phone despite there being no real need to charge it right away. Her husband, Finley, and six-year-old daughter, Lilias, were in Scotland visiting his parents for the summer. Sunny knew they were already asleep so there was no risk in missing a call from them, but she would be sure to call them after the funeral the following day. She anticipated this trip might test the limits of her anti-anxiety medication, but Finn had a knack for calming her nerves with only the sound of his voice.

Sunny hadn't visited her hometown in over ten years. The small community outside of Johnson City, Tennessee didn't offer much in the way of careers, so after attending school in Knoxville she made her way to New York City with Finley. He was a computer engineer and she was a writer. She wasn't sure how they ended up together since he was always so logical whereas she was the artistic and creative one. Perhaps that's *why* they worked so well together. They balanced each other out. Sunny visited her mother several times over the years, but ever since Willow moved to Knoxville there was never a reason to come back their hometown. Being back for her grandfather's funeral made her realize she should have made the trip over to see him when she was so close by. Instead she would call and apologize for not having enough time in her schedule. Even when her grandmother, Violet, died of breast cancer in 2005, she didn't make the trip home. Lilias was only two years old at the time and Finn had been away on a work trip. Asking her boss for more time off and traveling with a toddler by herself seemed impossibly overwhelming. Again, she called to apologize for not being able to make the trip. She was beginning to realize she might not have been a model granddaughter.

She found an outlet for her charger in the small sitting room. Before she could rejoin the other guests, her mother stepped in and closed the door behind her. Knowing she wasn't going anywhere for a few minutes, Sunny sat down in one of the armchairs. Willow sat down on the loveseat, laid back, and sighed.

"God almighty, I hate talkin' to all these old farts. Not one of 'em can hear me, so they lean in closer makin' me smell their God-awful breath. The old men try lookin' at my tits and maybe *accidentally* graze one as they go in for a hug, and the wives just judge me with their nasty ol' faces." Willow started to light a cigarette.

"Jesus, you're in rare form tonight. How much have you had to drink? And you know you can't smoke in here. It's not the nineties, mom."

"Oh, I haven't had anything yet. I cut way back in the last year or so. You'd be real proud of me if you ever visited or called." She looked at her daughter with a sarcastic smile and put her cigarettes away. "How was your trip home? Flight okay?"

"Yeah, it was fine. Not much traffic between here and Charlotte either."

"You been by the house yet?" Willow began fidgeting with the reading material on the table, straightening up the pile of tabloid magazines that appeared to be at least a decade old along with brochures on the grieving process.

"Nah. I came straight here. Didn't want to miss one second of this party, ya know?" Sunny smiled at her mom. She hadn't yet been able to gauge how stable Willow was on an emotional level.

"I figured you could stay there rather'n get a hotel room. Be a lot cheaper, but I guess money don't really matter when you got such a fancy job, huh?" Willow was truly proud of her daughter, but she had no idea how to express that feeling. It simply wasn't the way their family operated. "I have an appointment to meet daddy's lawyer there tomorrow after the funeral, so I'm stayin' over as well."

"Of course I'll stay there. A hotel never even crossed my mind. You think he left it to you? I mean, I can't imagine the farm would go to anyone else, right?"

"Hell, I don't know. That lawyer said somethin' on the phone about a specific request for the house and land. I guess we'll find out tomorrow." Willow stood up and adjusted her top so that her cleavage was more pronounced. She looked back at Sunny and winked, saying, "Gotta give the old men a thrill while they still got a pulse, eh?"

"Ugh! Come on, mom. That sentence alone will fill an entire session of therapy." As Sunny stood up, her bare arm brushed against a flower arrangement that was sitting on the side table. "*Ah shit!*" she exclaimed as a sharp pain caused her to jerk away quickly. She looked at the flowers while rubbing her arm and asked, "Who the hell sends a bouquet of petunias and thistle to a funeral?!"

"Welcome home, Sunny girl," Willow said, laughing as she left the room.

After departing the funeral home that evening, Sunny made her way down winding country roads to her grandparents' farm. It was a large Victorian-style house with a few barns and twenty acres of land. Sunny spent most of her life on the farm. Her childhood friends that lived in town were convinced that the house was haunted or that a witch lived there. She always found it quite comical that the other kids made up stories about the home she knew and loved. Of course, her wild imagination couldn't resist hinting at supernatural phenomena when they would ask her questions about it.

Pulling in the driveway in the dark, she couldn't see much of the house but from what she could tell it all looked the same. She got her suitcase out of the rental car and carried it onto the wrap-around porch. Lifting up the left side of the bench, she blindly felt around for the spare key and was delighted that it was still hidden in the same spot. Sunny took the key around to the side door that led into the kitchen and let herself in. She couldn't remember ever using the front door, despite the house having a beautiful entryway. As she stepped into the kitchen and turned on the light she realized nothing had changed. The house was exactly as she remembered it. The only relatively new appliance was the refrigerator and even that probably needed to be replaced.

Before she had a chance to wander through the house and stroll down memory lane, Willow pulled in the driveway. She carried in a pre-made casserole from one of the church ladies. A sticky note on the tinfoil cover stated to simply warm it up in the oven. Sunny sat at the kitchen table watching her mother. After putting the dish in the oven she opened the third cabinet from the stove and pulled out a bottle of vodka.

"I thought you stopped," Sunny said, raising an eyebrow.

Willow chuckled. "I can assure you, my darlin' child, those words ain't never come outta my mouth. I said I cut back." She took out two glasses from the dish drying rack near the sink and sat down at the table with her daughter. She began pouring.

"So how are you really doing, mom?"

"Oh, I'm alright, Sunny girl. How are you?" Classic deflection from Willow. Sunny knew it well.

"I'm good. Strange to think grampa's gone. I've never known this house without him."

"Yeah. Same for me. You know, I could tell the moment I walked in that day. I knew he was gone. He'd been sick with an awful cold or flu or somethin' for about a month. Every time I'd call and check on him he'd sound worse. Always told me to stop fussin' over him. I should have come to see him, but he just kept tellin' me he was fine. Said he had his friends here to look after him. Finally I told him enough is enough. Told him I's comin' on Saturday whether he liked it or not. Stubborn old man." Willow shook her head and scoffed. "Well, I called before I left Knoxville, but he didn't answer. When I got here his truck was still parked up by the barn like always. Like it is now. At first I thought maybe he's feelin' better and out workin' in the field. But I knew when I walked in here. The air felt... hollow." She took a drink and looked around the room. "Nothin' was outta the ordinary. Looked just like this, you know? Like it always has. I called out for him, but the words bounced off the walls differently. I walked upstairs to his bedroom and there he was, but I guess he wasn't really there at all."

"I'm so sorry, mom. That sounds terrifying." Sunny was surprised at how freely her mother was discussing her emotions. It was very much unlike her, and Sunny had no idea how to comfort her.

"No, baby. It wasn't terrifying. I mean, I's nervous walking up the stairs. I'm not entirely sure why. It was like that feelin' you get during the quiet part of a scary movie, right before the jump-scare. But when I saw him… there was a beauty to the whole thing. To go to bed one night and simply sleep the rest of your life away, we can only hope to be so lucky."

"That's a good way to look at it. I can't believe how many people were there tonight for the viewing. It was like the whole damn town. You must be exhausted from talking to them all."

"Well, it's not everyday the former mayor dies. Everyone wants to come pay their respects to the local celebrity and share their stories of the great Howard Richmond. Charity work this and church deacon that. He's a great man but it does get old after a while."

The oven timer beeped and seemed to jolt Willow out of her emotionally vulnerable state of mind. "Well, enough about all that. How's my grandbaby?"

"She's great. I don't think she really cares that I'm not over there with 'em right now. Finn's parents always spoil her. Oh, Finn sends his love."

"You know I'd rather hear it from him. I need to hear that sexy Scottish accent." She winked at Sunny.

"Jesus, mom. Why? Why do you have to go and say things like that?"

Willow laughed. "It's true! Ain't no sexy accents around here. Just a buncha hillbillies with no real sense about 'em. You got yourself a good one, Sunny girl."

"I know. He *is* a good one. And I agree that his accent is quite lovely." They laughed and clinked their glasses together.

Willow got up and pulled the casserole out of the oven. They sat and ate their late supper in silence. Sunny thought of Finn and Lil and how much she missed them. She was supposed to fly to Scotland the following week, and she was looking forward to the vacation. The only reason she wasn't with them already was because of a deadline she was up against for the magazine. She couldn't help but wonder if it was fate that she had to stay behind, because otherwise she wouldn't be with her mother in her childhood home. Willow, on the other hand, was thinking about the monumental task of cleaning a lifetime's worth of belongings from the house. She assumed the house would be left to her, but since she no longer lived there and had no intentions of moving back, her plan was to sell it. The money was much more appealing to her.

"Funeral starts at ten tomorrow mornin'. I told Max up at the funeral home we'd be there around nine. That okay?"

"Oh, gee, I don't know, mom. I had so many other plans for tomorrow. Of course it's fine. Do you want to just drive over together?"

"That'd be alright. I need to get back here at three to meet with daddy's lawyer. You remember Mr. Greenton, right. You'll stay for that won't you? I need someone smart in the room to make sure I ain't gettin' screwed over."

"Yep. My flight back to New York isn't for another two days."

"Two days? I get two whole days alone with my Sunny girl?! Well, ain't that a treat?" Willow smiled, genuinely excited to spend one-on-one time with her daughter after so many years apart.

"Ugh. Stop making me feel guilty for living outside of Tennessee. You know the planes and trains and highways all go *to* New York as well. It's not a one-way thing. I've told you a million times that I'll pay for your ticket, and yet you've still never visited me. Not once!" She was mostly teasing her mother, but part of her was truly disappointed that she'd never made the trip. Even after Lilias was born, Willow relied on phone calls and emailed photographs to get to know her granddaughter.

Willow threw a dish towel at Sunny and said, "Time for you to go to bed before I have to whoop your skinny ass! Go on. Get outta here. I'll clean up."

"Yes, ma'am." Sunny replied as if she were a surly teenager being sent to her room.

Walking up the grand staircase to her old bedroom, Sunny couldn't help but notice her muscle memory kicking in as she skipped the fourth step. She paused and smiled before stepping back down to hear the wood creak beneath her foot. She learned at an early age to skip that step if she wanted to go undetected during a game of hide-and-seek with her grandmother. The house smelled the same, looked the same, and sounded the same. But Willow was right. With her grandfather gone it didn't *feel* the same. She hung up her dress for the funeral next to some childhood graffiti still on the walls of her old closet. She unpacked her toiletries in the bathroom, noticing the rubber pig toy still sitting next to the bathtub in the same spot it had held for decades.

As she began to drift off to sleep in her old queen-size canopy bed, she heard her bedroom door open. Without lifting an eyelid, Sunny moved to the side and pulled back the covers. Willow slipped into bed and snuggled up to her daughter just as she had so many times before.

Willow had only been sixteen years old when she got pregnant, so Howard and Violet did more than their fair share of raising Sunny. Willow barely finished high school and always seemed to be more interested in socializing than creating a sustainable life for her and her young daughter. Because of that, Sunny had always been more of a friend or little sister to her. Willow knew she had failed as a mother in many ways, but the fact that Sunny was now independent, successful, and happy somehow made it all seem okay. She took comfort in the fact that despite being a less-than-ideal influence for her daughter, she knew she hadn't completely ruined her either.

"Night, mom."

"Goodnight, Sunny girl," she said, hugging her daughter tightly and grateful to not be alone in the house that held so many unpleasant memories.

Sunny looked in the full-length mirror and adjusted her dress before walking down to meet her mother. Willow was in the formal sitting room, which was at the bottom of the staircase. She was wearing a knee-length black dress with a pearl necklace and pacing across the room.

"You look really nice, mom." Sunny couldn't remember the last time she saw her mother dressed up for any occasion.

"Oh, hey. Thanks, baby. You look real good, too." She was speaking quickly while wringing her hands.

Sunny was suddenly on edge. "What's going on, mom? Everything okay? You feelin' alright?"

Willow kept pacing. "Yeah. I'm just tryin' real hard not to smoke a cigarette. I know you don't like it."

Sunny relaxed. "It's fine. These are extreme circumstances. You're allowed to use your favorite de-stressors. I won't judge."

"Oh thank God," she said with a heavy sigh. "Let's go. I'll roll the window down so we don't stink up your rental." She was already lighting a cigarette as Sunny linked her arm with her mother's and walked her to the car.

Much like the previous night, the funeral was well attended. By the time the preacher began the eulogy it was standing room only as people continued to slip in as quietly as they could. Sunny and Willow were sitting in the front row next to Howard's sister. Sunny had never met her before because she lived in California, and seeing as how their only connection was about to be buried she knew she'd never see her again. Sunny had to bite her cheek to keep from laughing when Willow leaned over whispering, "*I coulda swore she died years ago. Smells like her perfume is equal parts body odor and piss. Bless her heart.*" Willow winked at Sunny, knowing she'd understand why.

"*Stop it, mom! We are not blessing hearts right now. We're at grampa's funeral for Christ's sake,*" she scolded, still trying her best to keep from laughing. "Blessing Hearts" was a game Willow had made up a long time ago. It was one of the ways she tried to bond with her daughter when she wasn't sure what else to do. When Sunny was about twelve or thirteen years old, Willow would often take her to the mall on Saturday afternoons. The two of them would sit for hours in the food court, people watching and making snide comments to each other about the various shoppers. The more outrageous the comment, the better. They would always end their statements with "bless his heart" or "bless her heart" as a way to make their insults seem less cruel.

After the service at the funeral home the crowd made their way to the cemetery across town. It was a beautiful early summer day, and the graveside service was quite nice. The sun was warm, but there was a slight chill in the air. Howard's final resting place was in the middle of the cemetery next to his parents. Sunny wished her grandmother was buried there so that she could finally pay her respects, but Violet had asked to be cremated. Sunny realized she had no idea where her grandmother's ashes ended up and made a mental note to search for them back at the farmhouse.

Willow had instructed Sunny to park near the cemetery exit so that the car wouldn't be blocked by the crowd when it was time to leave. Once the group of people began quietly chatting as they slowly meandered away from Howard's final resting place, Sunny was stopped by her third grade teacher. She began talking with her about her life in New York and her job as a writer.

Willow began feeling somewhat anxious again and interrupted the old teacher, saying, "Excuse me, ma'am. Sunny girl, can you give me the keys? I need to grab a smoke before we get on over to the church. And don't forget we got to get back home in a bit to meet the lawyer." Sunny handed her the keys and continued talking with her former teacher.

As she made her way to the car, Willow passed by an elderly woman sitting on a bench near the walkway. She paid her no mind until she heard the woman speak.

"You are the willow, yes?" the slow, frail voice asked through an unusual accent.

Willow stopped and turned to look at her. She wasn't good at estimating people's ages, but she figured this woman had not only been alive for both world wars but had possibly fought in them as well. Her wrinkled skin had obviously weathered many storms. A colorful scarf was draped over her white hair, and an ornately carved cane leaned against her leg. Her presence was ghostly and enigmatic, sending a chill up Willow's spine.

"Excuse me?" Willow asked.

"You are the willow." She nodded with a sense of certainty, agreeing with herself.

Willow was already on edge from the day's events, and this woman was only making things worse. "Yeah. I mean, my name is Willow. Umm, are you here for my father, Howard?"

"No," the woman said quickly.

"Okay." Willow paused awkwardly. "Well, have a nice day."

Willow began walking away when the woman said, "I held you as a baby." She smiled without ever really looking at Willow. Instead she seemed to stare off into the distance.

Willow stopped and looked back over her shoulder. "Is that so? That... uhh... yeah, okay. Sure." She nodded and began looking around for someone that might be able to explain what exactly was happening or who this person was. "Were you friends with my parents?" She looked at the woman and thought about how old she might actually be and added, "Or maybe *their* parents?"

"The little sunflower is coming. I held her, too."

Willow turned and saw Sunny approaching. She looked back at the old woman and realized she hadn't actually looked in Sunny's direction before her last statement. Willow began feeling very uneasy and decided she needed a cigarette more than ever. "Okay, well it was lovely speaking with you, I guess." Sunny had caught up with her at this point and Willow turned to walk with her.

Still not breaking her distant gaze, the old lady said, "I will see you soon."

Sunny looked back at the old woman as she walked with her mother. "That grampa's lawyer?"

Willow chuckled at the idea. "Yeah, daddy's lawyer is some sort of cemetery goblin. I honestly don't know who or what that was. I'm just glad you saw her too. Creepy old thing for sure. I thought maybe she crawled outta one of these plots."

They drove to the First Baptist Church in town for the luncheon after leaving the cemetery. The church ladies had cooked an impressive meal for the guests and everyone seemed to be enjoying themselves. The melancholy from the funeral began to fade, making way for lively conversation and laughter.

"Daddy would have loved this," Willow said, looking around the crowded church basement where Sunday school classes were usually held. The beige, accordion room dividers had all been moved to the side, along with the small children's tables and chairs. The outer walls were covered with "Jesus loves you" posters and large hand-written lyrics for the children's choir practice. Well wishers wandered by Willow's table to offer their condolences and say hello to Sunny.

"It's almost two o'clock, mom. We need to be leaving soon if you want to get back home before the lawyer shows up." Sunny knew she'd have to keep an eye on the time. Willow was never one to leave a party early. They were able to make their way out of the church without getting cornered by any of the townsfolk. Both Sunny and Willow took off their high heels the moment they were in the car.

"Talkin' to all them people is just so damn draining. I don't know how you can do it." Willow began lighting a cigarette.

"Do what?"

"Live in a big city like New York with so many people around you all the time. It would make me a nervous wreck."

Sunny laughed. "Oh mom, that's the beauty of New York. You're surrounded by millions of people and yet you can feel totally alone. It's fantastic. And let me tell you, there are *so* many hearts in the city needin' to be blessed."

Once they arrived back at the house, Sunny was eager to call Finley and Lilias. It would be near dinnertime for them so she knew she would catch them before Lil went to bed. Hearing her daughter's voice was a wonderful break in an otherwise somber day.

"Mommy! Are you coming here tonight? I got to see a castle. A *real* castle!" Finley's parents were extremely wealthy, but Lilias was too young to understand. As far as she knew, everyone's grandparents owned a castle.

"Hi, Lil girl! That's so exciting about the castle! I wish I could've been there to see it with you, but I have to stay a few more days with Mamaw Willy."

"Bring Mamaw Willy to Scotland!" Lilias adored Willow and was beginning to realize she didn't get to see her as often as she'd like. "And bring some macaroni and cheese! The food here is kinda weird."

Sunny laughed. "Oh my, Lil. I'm not sure Mamaw Willy would ride on an airplane for that long. I'll see what I can do about the mac and cheese, though." She continued chatting with her daughter for a few more minutes, and then Finley got on the line.

"How's it goin', love? Have they had the funeral yet?"

She missed hearing his voice. It always calmed her no matter how high her anxiety and stress. "Hey, babe. Yeah, we just got back home. I'm staying at the old farmhouse with my mom."

"And how is she? Has she had any... uh, episodes?"

"Nah, nothing crazy yet. Hard to tell how she's really doing though. I mean, I know she's sad but I can't tell how dark she's gonna go now that the funeral is done and he's buried. Right now I feel like she's sort of going through the motions, you know? I'm staying here for a couple more days just to make sure she's stable." Sunny was all too familiar with her mother's mental health struggles of the past. Willow had battled with depression most of her life and was likely borderline bipolar, and nobody ever knew what would trigger her next breakdown.

"That's probably a good idea. When will you arrive here?"

"Umm, I think I'm back in the city for three days to finish packing and tying up some loose ends at the office, and then I fly out. I'll send you my itinerary once I get back to New York. How's everything going?"

"Not bad. Lilias is really eager to learn about our Scottish ways, and of course my maw and da are more than happy to talk about all the ancestors. We took her over to the estate today."

Sunny smiled. "I wish my side of the family was half as interesting as yours. We don't have any grand estates with castles. Of course, I used to think this farmhouse was a castle when I was a kid."

"*He just drove up, Sunny girl!*" Willow yelled from downstairs.

Finley had heard her calling and said, "Go on, love. Take care of yer maw, and call us in the morn if you get a chance."

"Alright. I love you, Finn. And give Lil a hug and kiss for me."

Sunny joined her mother downstairs on the porch to welcome their guest. Howard's lawyer, Mr. William Greenton, had arrived at the farmhouse at three o'clock sharp. Mr. Greenton had been a figure in Willow's life since she was a child, but she was surprised at how old he now appeared and wondered if he was thinking the same about her. They all sat at the formal dining room table with a pot of coffee and some leftover appetizers Sunny had swiped before they left the church luncheon. Mr. Greenton took a stack of papers out of his briefcase and began organizing them into various piles and folders.

"Well, Willow, your father's estate is pretty straight forward, and since you are an only child I don't foresee any disputes with Howard's final wishes."

Willow smiled and glanced over at Sunny. "That's good to hear, Mr. Greenton. You mentioned something on the phone about a specific request. What was—"

"Oh yes, of course. Essentially, it boils down to the fact that you are to keep the farmhouse and land in the family." Mr. Greenton continued organizing the stack of papers and lining up documents for Willow to sign.

"What the fuck?! Are you sayin' I can't sell this place?!" Willow shouted, startling the lawyer.

"Whoa! Mom, calm down. No need to yell at him. He's just telling you what grampa wanted."

"I'm really sorry for upsetting you, Willow. The land, the house, and all the contents within it were left to you, and it is imperative that you do not sell it. I mean, legally you *can* sell it once you own it, but I would strongly caution against doing anything rash." He had been turning the documents around so that they were facing Willow, and he carefully slid a pen across the table to her. "All that's left to do is just sign a few of these papers. I've put the little sticky arrows so that you see where —"

"I see it just fine," Willow snapped. She began signing, cursing her deceased father and his lawyer under her breath.

Sunny looked at Mr. Greenton, smiled apologetically, and nodded as if to say, *This is all totally fine and normal. Don't take it personally.*

Once the paperwork had been completed and Mr. Greenton had left the house, Willow and Sunny sat silently at the table. Sunny knew Willow was in a fragile state, teetering on the verge of a complete collapse. Selling the house had been the plan all along, and it made sense as it would give Willow a much needed financial cushion that she had never been able to accumulate on her own.

Sunny was the first to break the silence. "So what now, mom? How can I help?"

Willow simply shook her head and said, "I don't know. I truly don't know. I mean, where do I even begin? Do I just start throwing things away? Do I set up a big ass yard sale? Do I just lock the door and leave it all like it is?"

Sunny noticed her mother was wringing her hands again. "You want a cigarette, mom? Or I could get you a drink if you think that might help."

"Yeah, go get that vodka. I'll be able to think better with a buzz."

Sunny went to the kitchen and came back with the bottle and two glasses. She wasn't planning on driving anywhere that evening, so she saw no reason she couldn't have a drink as well. She needed to slow her mind down and alcohol seemed like as good a solution as any.

"How do you empty a house this big? It's full of all kinds of shit. And that's what it all is — Shit. Ain't nothing here worth any money. Mama Vi wouldn't have that. Couldn't ever spend a few extra dollars for somethin' nice. No! All of daddy's hard earned money had to go straight into the bank." It wasn't unlike Willow to rail against her mother. Sunny was quite used to it, and she knew she had to let her vent once she started. "You know, if she wanted to save money so bad she should have gotten her own goddamn job. And all that money that daddy saved up, where do you think it went? To her own dang chemo treatments. Ain't nothin' left for me except this house and all the shit they stored in it." She turned up her glass, finishing what was left in it, and began pouring another. "How am I gonna get through all this by myself, Sun? How?"

"I'm here for a couple more days, mom. I'll help you work out a plan and figure out a process that'll get you through all of it without overwhelming you. Okay?" Often Sunny would have to take charge and act as the adult when her mother fell into this state of mind, especially when Violet's name came up.

"*I'm already overwhelmed and I ain't even done nothin' yet!*" she shouted.

"Christ, mom! I'm sitting right here! No need to scream!" Sunny said in an obscenely loud voice. Humor and sarcasm could usually break the tension, so Sunny had developed a quick wit over the years. She lowered her voice and said calmly, "Why don't we just walk around and take a mental inventory? That won't be hard, right? We can find things that are obviously trash, things that we could sell, and things we could donate. Then we'll have an idea of how big this job really is, okay?"

Willow rolled her eyes. "I hate that you're so goddamn sensible and calm all the time. Sure as hell didn't inherit that from me."

Sunny smiled, happy knowing she had gained control of the situation. "Alright. Where should we start?"

Though the old Victorian house looked huge from the outside, it was only two stories. There was no basement and the attic had always been empty. There were four bedrooms and one full bathroom on the second floor. The main level of the house was made up of the formal sitting room and entryway at the bottom of the steps, the formal dining room, the living room, the study, the powder room, the kitchen, and the walk-in pantry. Willow decided the easiest place to start their mental inventory was the sitting room.

Sunny sat down on the small wooden bench at the upright piano and asked, "Think we should sell this?" She played a few keys at random and smiled.

"I sure as hell don't want to keep it. Mama never even let me play it," Willow said harshly.

"Really? That's weird." Not wanting to hear another rant about Violet, Sunny stood up and gestured to the antique red velvet couch. "Ok, well what about this? I always thought this was the fanciest piece of furniture in the world."

Willow smiled. "Oh me too. I always loved this couch. I think I want to keep that."

"Okay! See? We're already making progress. Do any of these pictures or end tables or anything have significant value to you?" The sitting room was by far the easiest room since it was only decorative furnishings.

Willow looked around the room. "Honestly, I never really noticed any of it. It can all be dona— Actually, no. I'd rather sell it and get some money for it."

"Boom! One room down. Keep the couch and sell the rest. Easy enough." Sunny looked back at the piano. "And to be honest, I might buy the piano. It would be good for Lil to learn."

"Surely they sell pianos in New York City. Why the hell would you buy this one and have to figure out how to get it there?" Willow was looking at her daughter as if she'd lost her mind.

"I'm assuming you'll give me a good deal on this one. Everything is so expensive in the city, you know? I think even with shipping it would be cheaper to just buy this one from you." It wasn't the whole truth, but Sunny figured she would try and stick to the task at hand.

"Fine. Make it my Christmas gift to Lil. Now you just have to pay for movin' it up there." Willow was happy to get rid of it and knowing she was also making her granddaughter happy made it that much better.

They made their way from the sitting room to the dining room, walking under the decorative crown molding that separated the two. Looking at it now, Sunny realized how delicately the wood had been hand-carved and customized for that space back in the late 1800s. There was an "R" carved out of the center, and in a way Sunny agreed with her grandfather that the house should stay in the family. It had always been owned by the Richmonds, something Howard liked to remind everyone, and there was a sense of pride that went along with that.

The dining room would be nearly as simple as the sitting room. The table and chairs would be donated. Willow figured there were too many scrapes and scuffs and stains on the wood to sell it. The only other piece of furniture in the room was the large hutch which had always displayed many pieces of depression-era glass, ceramic dishes, and porcelain animal figurines. The drawers held the "fancy" silverware that was only used on special occasions, and the cabinets at the bottom were filled with old tablecloths, aprons, cloth napkins, and placemats for every season and holiday.

"That's all mama's. Put it in the for-sale pile."

"Really? Oh come on. You don't want to keep *anything* of mamaw's? I mean, those dishes are super old. Like family heirlooms. You're just going to get rid of them?" Sunny was starting to feel somewhat sad and frustrated by this process. Though she hadn't been to the house in many years, she still felt a deep connection to it and to the belongings within it, but her desire to keep her mother sane was far outweighing her emotions and nostalgia.

"I'd rather have the money than the memories of her. I don't think you understand what it was like to grow up in this house with a mom like her." Willow walked out of the room and into the kitchen. Sunny couldn't help but look at the colorful glass dishes and porcelain animals for a few moments more. Her eyes grew wide when she noticed the small puppy figurine in the back corner. Violet had told her it was a magical puppy that brought joy to anyone who was feeling sad. Whenever Sunny would cry as a young girl she would hold onto the puppy, and it never failed to make her feel better. Reaching into the hutch, she pulled out the puppy and stuck it in her pocket for safe keeping. The fact was that she *had* grown up in the house with Violet for many years, but she obviously had a very different experience than her mother. And it was an experience Willow was never interested in hearing.

The powder room and pantry went quickly with Willow simply saying, "Donate it all. Ain't nothin' worth money in here." Sunny began fearing that her mother was getting tired of this process and simply giving up, so when they hit the kitchen she decided it was time for a well deserved break.

"Let's see if grampa left anything good in the freezer." Sunny walked over and pulled out a tub of vanilla ice cream. She looked at the container and excitedly proclaimed, "Holy shit. It's *not* expired!" Looking in the refrigerator she found chocolate syrup, also not yet expired. Willow had already started getting the bowls and spoons. "He's got a frozen pizza in there. Want me to cook that for supper?"

"Yeah, that'd be fine. The pizza can be our dessert." Willow smiled like a child who was sneaking into the cookie jar before suppertime as she scooped out her ice cream.

It was hard for Sunny not to see her mother as an equal or even as a younger sister. There were so many times in her life she had to be the adult in situations when Willow was in a bad way, especially after they moved out of the farmhouse. Except for a brief period when she was four or five years old, Sunny had never lived anywhere other than the farmhouse. When she turned twelve years old, Willow started renting a trailer in town and decided it was time she became a full-time mom. Sunny hadn't wanted to leave the farmhouse and her grandparents, but Willow had assured her that every night would be like a slumber party in their new home. For the next six years she would bounce between the farmhouse and whatever trailer or apartment her mother was living in. Once she turned eighteen, she left for college and never looked back.

Seeing her mother so vulnerable again was bringing back a lot of hard memories. She was beginning to remember how exhausting it was to be close to Willow for an extended period of time, and she'd only been home for one day. Pushing past her own feelings, she knew getting a plan in place for her mother was the only option at this point. Otherwise she knew the farmhouse would simply be locked up and left to the elements. She had two days to get as much accomplished as possible.

With the pizza in the oven, they had twenty minutes to get through the living room and the study. Willow was pretty quick to call out things for sale or donate in the living room. It was all old furniture that she wasn't necessarily interested in, but the knick-knacks were a different story. A candle that was a small hollowed-out tree trunk was something she wanted to keep. Sunny asked her where it came from.

"I don't really know. It's just always been here and I remember likin' it when I's a kid. I thought it was somethin' special to have a piece of a tree like that sitting on the table." Willow wasn't sure why she liked it so much. If she was being perfectly honest she'd forgotten all about it until that moment, but suddenly she couldn't imagine letting it go. She found several things in the living room like that and she figured it was because that's where she'd spent the most time as a kid. A large marble ashtray sat on the center of the coffee table. This was another piece she couldn't bear to part with now that she'd seen it again.

Except for the powder room, the study was the only room on the main floor of the house that had a door so that it could be closed off. Sunny had no memories of this room because she never really went in there as a child. The fireplace in the corner had the most beautiful mosaic-tiled mantle. She couldn't help but think how it would be another unique architectural piece lost forever if they sold the house. Sunny ran her fingers along the faded and peeling wallpaper as she looked at the bookshelves. They were covered in so many cobwebs and so much dust she couldn't even read the titles of the books. An old record player sat on a table near the window. It too was covered in dust and cobwebs. Next to it was a faded record sleeve. Sunny picked it up and blew the top layers of dust away, revealing the title *(Oh My Darling) Clementine*. She wondered if this was something her mother listened to as a child and was about to ask when she realized it would have to wait.

Willow was crying. The sight of Howard's pipe sitting on the desk next to a pencil and a newspaper opened to the unfinished crossword puzzle was more than she was prepared for. She sat in the desk chair holding her hands to her face. She tried to hold back her tears, but she couldn't.

"It's okay, mom. I know this is hard. How about we just leave this room for last. Or maybe we just say this whole room is on the keep list until you have more time to really look through it." Sunny began feeling ashamed of herself, realizing she was having her mother go through the house mere hours after burying her father. She paused and let Willow catch her breath and dry her eyes. "I'm going to go check on the pizza. I'll let you know when it's ready." She paused as she walked out of the room. "I'm really sorry, mom."

"Yeah, it's okay. That sounds good, baby. I'm just gonna sit here for a few more minutes." She smiled, but there was no hiding her sorrow.

Willow had always been a daddy's girl. She adored and idolized Howard her entire life. Her mind wandered back to her childhood when she would run around the farm while Howard worked in the barn. She gladly helped him with chores and followed him, mimicking his every move. Willow hated having to spend time at home alone with her mother whenever Howard would go into town for work. Often she would chase his truck down the driveway, desperate for him to take her along. She would wait for him on the porch swing for so long that eventually she'd fall asleep.

Around the time Willow entered junior high school Howard was elected mayor of their small town. She took this as a sign that her family was now as good as royalty and assumed she was above the law. A few times she was caught trying to steal candy from the dollar store, and as she got a bit older it turned into swiping cigarettes and small bottles of liquor. Howard could always make the problems go away by calling up the sheriff or talking to the store owners and paying for whatever she had taken. If that didn't work, Mr. Greenton could always get her charges dropped. Willow believed that she could do no wrong in her father's eyes and that he would always be there to get her out of a jam. Then she discovered she was pregnant. That forever changed her relationship with Howard, and Willow's behavior and emotional stability had been spiraling ever since.

"Pizza's ready, mom!" she heard Sunny shout from the kitchen. She looked around the study once more and then joined her daughter for supper.

Walking into the kitchen she said, "I'm not sure what the hell just happened to me in there. I had the strongest feeling of… I don't even know what to call it. Like I was safe from all the world. Like nothin' could hurt me."

"Maybe you felt grampa's spirit in there. Do you have lots of memories of him working at his desk when you were little?" Sunny smiled at the thought of her mom being a child and of her grandparents as young adults.

"Not really. I mean, daddy never used that as his office or anything. It's such a strange sensation now that I think about it. When I's a kid I don't think I ever remember him bein' in there at all. Mama would keep flowers on the window sill, but other'n that I don't think anyone ever used the study." Willow paused, searching for an explanation to why she had such a strong reaction to being in that room. Not finding one, she shrugged her shoulders and began slicing the pizza. "I guess we'll start looking at the upstairs next, huh?"

"Oh, no. We don't have to, mom. I know this is a lot to do so quickly. I'm fine with waiting until tomor—"

Willow was already shaking her head. "Nope. Let's get this done. We're making progress, Sunny girl! Damn good progress! I do, however, need more fuel for the fire. Where's the vodka?"

The upstairs was a long hallway with doors on each side. The bathroom was at the end of the hallway near the narrow spiral staircase that led to the pantry down by the kitchen. Sunny always thought this was a secret passageway that only she knew about because she never saw the adults use it. She liked to sneak down to get snacks after her bedtime while her grandparents were still awake. It was always a thrill when she would succeed and not get caught.

The first door on the right in the hallway was Willow's old bedroom. "I think we can skip this one. I know what's in here. It's all my stuff, and I'll deal with it later." With that Willow shut the door and continued to the next door, which was Sunny's old room across the hall on the left. She opened the door, gestured to her daughter, and smiled saying, "I'm guessing everything in here is yours. So *you* can deal with all that."

Sunny smirked. "Fantastic."

The next door on the right was the master bedroom. Sunny braced for Willow's reaction since this was where she had found Howard's body less than a week before. To her surprise she didn't seem affected at all. Instead, Willow pointed at the bed and joked, "I'm going to recommend trashing the sheets and blankets. Ain't nobody wants to buy bedding that's full of death." Sunny knew the vodka was doing its job, but this would have to be Willow's last one for the evening. One more drink and she would likely take a dark turn. Over the years Sunny had developed an ability for determining when her mother needed to be cut off from alcohol. It wasn't a talent she was proud of, but it had been a necessary skill for her as a child.

Sunny opened the closet door and then looked in the dresser drawers. "Well, it looks like grampa already cleaned out everything of mamaw's. So that makes it easier, huh?"

Willow laughed and then stared at her daughter with a confused look on her face. "Wait. Are you serious right now?"

"What? I mean, all her clothes are gone. So that's one less thing for you to deal with, right?" Sunny wasn't sure what her mother was asking.

Willow began laughing again as if she couldn't believe what she was hearing. She raised her hands in the air, danced around, and laughed while yelling, *"Oh my God, Sunny girl! You are the sweetest, most naive little girl that ever lived!"*

"What the hell, mom? I don't get it. What'd I do?" Sunny was beginning to think maybe her mother had one drink too many after all.

Willow didn't respond. She simply walked out of the room and down the hall to the last door before the bathroom. Sunny followed her, slightly annoyed that her mother wasn't answering her. Willow opened what Sunny had always believed to be a storage room.

Instead, she found a fully decorated bedroom that obviously hadn't been touched in years.

"What the—Who's room is this?" Sunny began looking around. She opened the closet to find a full wardrobe hanging up. "Are these mamaw's clothes? Did grampa move all her stuff in here after she died? I don't understand."

Willow scoffed. "*After* she died? Sunny, they stopped sharing a room when I's in high school."

"*What?!* No way!" Sunny was laughing at the absurdity of her mother's statement. "There's no way I wouldn't notice them living in different rooms. That's ridiculous."

"Not sure what to tell you, kid. She moved over here at some point. They never talked about it, though. I never asked. I just assumed she was gonna leave him and get a divorce, but that never happened."

Sunny was stunned. How could she have not noticed something like that? Her mind started racing trying to find any sort of repressed memory that would help it all make sense, but she couldn't think of any. "I... I don't even know what to say right now."

"I can't believe you didn't know they had separate rooms. Jesus Christ, girl." Willow walked out of the room and back down the hallway. Sunny followed her, scratching her head and still looking back at the somewhat secretive bedroom. "I'm gonna go back down and eat another slice of that pizza and see if anything's on the TV."

Sunny was confused, sad, a little angry, and most of all, tired. "I think I'm just gonna call it a night. We got through most of the house, but this," she said gesturing to the separate rooms, "this is just too much for my brain to handle. My mind is totally blown right now."

"Alrighty. Goodnight, baby." As Willow began walking down the stairs she shouted back over her shoulder, "I sure don't know how the hell you missed that. You crack me up, Sunny girl."

"Goodnight, mom. And stop making fun! It's not nice!"

She heard Willow laugh before calling out, "Bless your heart, baby girl!"

"*You're such a dick, mom!*" she shouted back, getting the last word in. This only made Willow laugh harder.

Sunny walked into her room and shut the door. She sat on the edge of her bed and looked around her room, wondering how she could have been so clueless. She wanted to know why, hoping that it was as simple as the fact that her grandfather snored loudly. But something in the back of her mind told her there was much more to the story.

Sunny woke from a dreamless sleep, but her mind instantly filled with questions about her grandparents. It was shortly after eight o'clock, and she knew her mother would still be asleep. She decided to call Finn and Lil to get her morning started off on a positive note. She explained to him that her short visit to Tennessee would be busier than she'd expected because of the situation with the house. Organizing and planning a job this large would be exhausting, but Sunny was up for the challenge. Plus, she felt she had no choice but to help her mother.

After hanging up the phone and without getting out of her bed, Sunny shouted for Willow. "*Mom! You awake?!*" She waited, and then followed up with, "*MOM! GET UP!*" She waited again, but this time she heard Willow's feet hit the floor and stomp across the hall before opening the bedroom door.

"Are you kidding me right now? You want breakfast in bed or somethin'?" Willow had never been a morning person.

"Just wanted to say good mornin', mom!" Sunny said with a grin.

"Oh, shut up." With that, Willow turned and walked down the hall to the bathroom. Sunny got up and headed to the kitchen to start the coffee.

Once Willow joined her and sat down at the table Sunny wasted no time in getting the day started. "So why the separate rooms? Did grampa snore? Did mamaw snore? How did they keep it a secret? *Why* did they keep it a secret? When did—"

"For God's sake, Sun! What's with the rapid-fire interrogation?"

"This is a huge deal for me! It's like my entire childhood was a lie. I mean, they're kind of my only family except for you, so I'd like to know their history. This has rocked my world, mom!" She was feeling less sad and angry and more curious and excited to solve a mystery. "To be honest, I don't know much about them at all. Now I'm intrigued."

"So you wait until they're both dead to be *intrigued*? Nice timing, kid." Willow chuckled. She took a drink of her coffee, looked out the screen door to the porch, took a deep breath and said, "Well, I can tell you what I know, but I'm sure it ain't nothin' I haven't told you before. Daddy worked a lot, either here on the farm or in town. Mama didn't do shit except work in her garden or putter around the house. I had to wear second-hand clothing 'cause she'd never buy me new things. She wouldn't let me go out with friends or nothin'. Daddy'd let me help him around the farm. He'd give me a few dollars for each birthday and tell me to hide it from mama so that she wouldn't take it. And then there was the time that she—"

"Okay, you know what? If this is just gonna be another bitch session about mamaw I don't want to hear it. We've got a lot of work to do today." Sunny stood up and began clearing the table. "How about you work on grampa's room and I'll take mamaw's?"

Sunny could hear her mother moving things around in the master bedroom across the hall. Willow was eager to get some progress made on clearing out the house. Sunny, on the other hand, was still trying to understand why her grandmother, Violet, had a separate bedroom. It wasn't just that they slept in separate rooms. It was more like they had completely separated their lives. There was nothing of hers in the master bedroom and nothing of his in the "guest" room. From the looks of things, Howard had never entered this room even after Violet passed away. There were flower pots on the window sill still filled with soil, but the flowers that had once bloomed there were long gone.

She started in the closet. There were several dresses she recognized from her childhood such as the "fancy" dresses that Violet would wear to church during Easter or Christmas services. She remembered going to church with her so many years ago. Violet would always give her a quarter to put in the collection plate. Sunny never actually liked going to church. It was a constant struggle to stay awake during the boring sermons. Yet there was something about it she missed. Perhaps it was the routines and traditions or the songs and uncomfortable pews. Maybe it was simply her grandmother that she missed.

In the closet she also found shoeboxes full of newspaper clippings. It seemed like anytime a relative's name showed up in print Violet would cut it out and save it. Along with the various articles that mentioned the family were dozens of obituaries for people Sunny had never heard of. There were also church programs from holidays long ago, Bible verses printed on bookmarks, and one box was filled with hand-written recipe cards, labeled: *From Mom*. Sunny knew the contents of that box was something she would want to keep.

In the very back of the closet were two more boxes, one labeled "Sunny" and the other labeled "Willow". To her surprise she found all of her old school work, drawings, report cards, crafts, and about two dozen participation ribbons from various events. Looking in Willow's box was nearly the same with all of her school papers, finger paintings, stories she'd written, and notebooks filled with drawings. Violet had kept it all. Sunny wondered if her mother had any idea that the woman she had once deemed "pure evil" had such a sentimental side to her.

Next she moved to the roll-top desk that was in the corner of the bedroom. Upon opening the desktop, she found old stationary with her grandmother's initials, blank envelopes, a book of stamps, and a small photo of Sunny from the second grade. It was a wallet-sized photo in a small but decorative frame. She smiled as she picked it up to get a closer look. Something was strange about it, though. It felt bulkier than a normal photo in a frame. She turned it over and opened the back of it. A small key fell onto the desk.

She gasped and whispered to herself, "*A secret key.*" Picking it up, she stopped whispering and began shouting, "*Mom! Oh my God! Hurry! I found a secret key!*"

Willow stuck her head in the room and asked, "What in God's name are you hollerin' about?"

"Mamaw had a *secret key* hidden behind *my* picture!" Sunny hadn't been this excited in years. As a child she was always looking for adventure, and finding a hidden key was exactly the kind of thing she always dreamed about. "What do you think it opens?!"

Willow walked in and took the key from her. She turned it in her hand as she looked at it. There were no identifying marks on it. "No idea, Sunny girl. Probably an old diary or something."

"No way. Nuh-uh. That's too big to be a diary key. Maybe it's to a treasure chest or something!"

Willow cocked her head to the side and asked, "A treasure chest? She wasn't a fuckin' pirate. What's the matter with you?"

As Willow began to leave the room Sunny looked back at the picture frame the key had fallen out of. She noticed faded writing on the back of her school photo. Upon closer inspection she read aloud, "Knoxville Federal."

Willow abruptly stopped in the doorway, turned around quickly, and yelled, "*Holy shit! It's a safety deposit box!*"

Sunny's eyes got wide as she looked back at the key and whispered, "*So it* is *a treasure chest.*" She then jumped up and they both began celebrating the mystery key and whatever it might lead to.

Willow headed for the door and called out over her shoulder, "Get yer shit together, Sunny girl. We're goin' to Knoxville!"

They arrived at the bank in Knoxville a little before lunchtime. During the hour and a half drive Willow contemplated what they might find at the bank. "Maybe it's my *true* inheritance. Like, maybe all that money she had daddy save so long ago was put into one of them CDs or stocks or somethin'.." Sunny didn't really care what was in the box. She was just there to solve the mystery. It was the perfect way to keep her mother occupied and not overwhelmed with going through the house. Plus she couldn't wait to tell Lilias all about the adventure of the secret key.

Now that Lilias was old enough to understand that adults had jobs and that her mother was a writer, she always begged for Sunny to write stories for her. They were always short, adventurous tales where the lead character was a strong, brave, smart young girl who always looked a lot like Lilias. Sunny loved writing these stories and empowering her daughter, but she had been toying with the idea of writing a more realistic story for when she was older. Lilias had become very interested in family history, and this summer's trip to Scotland was going to focus on learning about Finn's family. Sunny had been somewhat panicked because she didn't know much about her own family, and now it seemed she knew nothing about them. She hoped finding this secret key would help her write the story of her ancestry. If nothing else, it would make an excellent start to another bedtime fairytale.

When they arrived at the bank, the lady behind the counter was a very plump woman in her late fifties. She seemed friendly and had nothing but smiles for the guests in her line. The other teller behind the counter looked much more disgruntled and annoyed. Sunny chose the plump woman's line. She wasn't sure if they would have trouble getting into the safety deposit box since neither of them were the actual owners of the key and she would much rather deal with a nice person in that situation. Her name was Agnes according to the placard in front of her window, and she acted as though working at the bank was the biggest blessing of her life.

"Welcome to the Knoxville Federal Savings and Loan! How can I help you two lovely ladies today?"

Before Willow could say anything, Sunny spoke up. "Hi there, Agnes. We absolutely need your help today. You see, my grandmother passed away several years ago, and—"

"Oh, darlin'. I'm so sorry to hear that. Bless your heart, and God rest her soul." Willow snickered at this heartfelt response from Agnes, but Sunny ignored her.

"Uhh, yes. Thank you. Umm, anyway... We found a key that we think belongs to a safety deposit box here. Is that something you can help us with?" She was holding the key out for Agnes to see.

"Well, that does look like one of ours. Can I get a name for the account that it's attached to? And then I'll of course need your names and some ID. Can't never be too careful, ya know? Lots of crazies in this world." Agnes was very animated while she talked.

"Of course. Thank you, Agnes. The account would belong to Violet Richmond. That's my grandma's name. Oh, and this is my mother," she said, gesturing toward her. "Willow Richmond." Willow smiled at Agnes and waved. Sunny whispered to her, "Get your ID out."

Typing and staring at the monitor of her computer, Agnes furrowed her brow. "I'm not seeing that name in our system. Is there another name it might be under?"

"Try Howard Richmond. That was her husband, my grandfather," Sunny replied.

Again, Agnes was unsuccessful in finding the account. "No, dear. I'm afraid that isn't in here either."

"Try Rose. Violet Rose. That was her maiden name," Willow said from behind Sunny.

Agnes continued pounding away at the keyboard and began to nod her head. She asked a few more questions about addresses and birthdates. Eventually she cheerfully said, "Ah, here we are! We do indeed have a box belonging to Violet Rose. Now there are three other names on the account, and one of those is Miss Willow Richmond." She looked at Willow and asked with a sincere smile, "Can I see that ID now, sugar?"

Willow handed it to her as Sunny asked, "Can you tell us who the other names are on the account?"

Agnes studied Willow's drivers license and typed a few more things before returning it to her. "Yes, ma'am, I surely can. Looks like the other names on here are a Miss Sunflower Richmond—oh my, what a name, huh?"

Sunny looked at Willow accusingly and said, "Yeah, it's somethin' alright." Willow smiled back at her and shrugged.

Agnes continued, "—and a Miss Maisy Edwards. Okay, I think we've got everything in order here. I can take y'all back to the boxes now." Agnes left her post at the teller's desk and walked around the counter. Willow and Sunny followed her to a secured room on the opposite side of the bank's foyer.

As Agnes fumbled with multiple keys to unlock the doors, Sunny whispered to her mother, "Grampa's name isn't on the account. That's weird, right?"

Willow, always skeptical of her mother, replied, "Hard tellin' what she's been hidin' in here."

They watched as Agnes pulled down box 204 and placed it on a table in the center of the room. "Is there anything else I can help you two ladies with today?"

"No, ma'am. You've been just wonderful, Agnes. Thank you so much for your help." Sunny was genuinely impressed with Agnes. After years of dealing with the hustle and bustle of New Yorkers, she forgot how overly friendly and patient southerners could be.

Agnes left them alone in the room with the mystery box and secret key. Willow was eager to look inside to see what sort of valuables might be awaiting her. Sunny opened the box revealing a stack of papers, envelopes, and a small box. She could tell her mother was somewhat disappointed it wasn't overflowing with diamonds and gold. Willow began shuffling through the papers and seemed to be getting angrier by the second. Next she pulled out the envelopes of handwritten letters. At the bottom of the box were a few faded black and white photographs which Willow simply tossed aside. Lastly, she grabbed the small box. Inside was a rectangular amethyst ring with a gold rose inlaid in the center. Sunny admired its beauty, while Willow could only try and estimate how much she could get for it at a pawn shop.

"Couple hundred bucks at least, don't you think?" Willow asked, studying the ring.

"Huh? No! You can't sell it, mom!" Sunny took it from her and began inspecting it. The gem from the center of the rose was missing, but other than that it was perfect. A true family heirloom that Sunny wanted to know more about.

Willow snatched it back from her. "The hell I can't. If I'm being guilted into not selling the farm you can bet yer ass I'm sellin' everything else I can."

"Fine, mom," Sunny replied with a sigh. "I'll buy it from you. How's that?"

"Whatever." With the safety deposit box now empty, Willow felt defeated. She stared at the empty box, clenched her jaw, and quietly said, "That's it. That's all she left me. Some papers, some junk mail, some pictures of people I don't even know, and a ring that looks like it came outta the quarter machine out in front of the five and dime. Real nice, mama. Just great. So fucking on brand for her." Willow had convinced herself on the car ride over to Knoxville that this treasure would change everything. Instead, she felt deceived and embarrassed. "I'm gonna go tell ol' Agnes that we're ready to leave. You can throw all that stuff out. I don't care. Let's just get back to the farm and clear the shit outta the house and be done with it." Willow tossed the ring onto the table and left the room.

Sunny looked at everything laying before her more curious than ever. Her mother might have given up, but the number of questions she had about her grandmother had grown exponentially since the moment they opened the box, and Sunny just couldn't walk away from a good mystery. As she gathered up the papers, photographs, and envelopes she noticed the return addresses all had the same name.

"*Maisy Edwards*," she whispered to herself. Though she'd heard that name only minutes before, it took a moment for her to place it. "*The other name on the account. Well now Miss Maisy, who the hell are you?*"

They stopped for lunch on their way out of Knoxville, but there wasn't much in the way of conversation. Sunny could tell Willow was disappointed and not in the mood to talk. The car ride was equally as silent as Willow stared out the window, periodically wringing her hands. Her mind was working overtime with scenarios where she was able to tell her mom how disappointed she was with her. And now these thoughts began to include telling off her father, which had never happened before, but the fact that he was making her keep the house was too much. She was angry with him, and she didn't know how to handle that feeling while also grieving for him.

When they arrived back at the farmhouse it was late afternoon, and Willow went straight upstairs to continue clearing out Howard's room. Sunny went to the dining room table to begin looking through the contents of the safety deposit box. The photographs were no help. Most were of two young women, often standing side by side and smiling for the camera. She knew one of the girls was her grandmother, and so she could only assume the other was Maisy. Hoping to solve the mystery quickly, she decided the letters would be her best bet. Sunny had always been fascinated with old letters. She couldn't remember the last time she'd written or received a hand-written letter, and with cursive writing becoming a lost art, these letters were even more charming.

The first strange thing Sunny noticed was that the letters weren't addressed to the farmhouse. They had been mailed to a P.O. box in a town nearly thirty minutes away. As far as Sunny knew, her grandmother had never lived anywhere else. She realized she needed to stop assuming she knew anything about her grandparents at this point, because it was becoming painfully evident that she knew nothing about them at all.

Based on the contents of the letters it was clear that Maisy had been a friend of her grandmother's. Nothing led her to believe she was related to either Violet or Howard. These letters, which were dated in the late sixties and seventies, were sometimes about the weather or current news stories but mostly they were filled with information about flower arrangements and tips for gardening such as: *the forget-me-nots will grow best on the banks of the creek; lavender should not be planted near the roses; heather would look beautiful in and around the house; ferns pair well with anemones;* and *camellias might thrive if planted near the dogwoods.*

Sunny thought back to her childhood and could almost smell the flowers that filled the window sills of every room in the house. Violet also had a stunning flower garden near the old milking barn. She would spend hours out there during the day sitting on a bench and reading books or simply admiring the flowers. Sometimes Sunny would join her and listen to her grandmother name each type of flower. She wished she could remember what they were, but she had only been three or four years old at the time. Sunny thought Maisy could have been a member of the old gardening club Violet was a part of, but that wouldn't explain why she owned a safety deposit box with her.

Sunny was feeling slightly frustrated with the lack of clarity from the letters and photographs, so she began eyeing the stack of documents that had also been in the box. The first was about the Victorian farmhouse, and Sunny was captivated by what she read. Not only did it detail the ownership history of the house, but it laid out a family tree she had never seen before.

The home was built for Harry and Cynthia Rose in 1897. Harry was a retired logger and Cynthia had been a school teacher. They had nine children, the youngest of which, a son named John, was nearly a teenager when they moved to the new farmhouse. John grew up and married Margaret Holman in 1908. John and Margaret inherited the farmhouse as a wedding gift from his parents, with the understanding that Harry and Cynthia would live out their days on the farm. John and Margaret were eager to start a family, and welcomed their daughter, Cora, in 1910.

Sadly, Margaret died shortly after Cora's birth and John never remarried. Cora Rose grew up and married Dee Wilson in 1934, and ownership of the house changed to her name. The Wilsons had a daughter in 1935, but Dee left Cora for another woman in 1938. Cora was devastated to lose the man she thought had been the love of her life. After spending a few weeks at home alone with her young daughter, she decided to go to the courthouse and change her and her daughter's name back to Rose. She no longer wanted the Wilson name to cast a shadow on their lives. Cora raised her daughter on her own, and never remarried. She once came close with a man named Dale, but he left for WWII and never returned. The last entry in the ownership document was from 1955 when Cora gifted the farmhouse to her only child, Violet Rose.

Sunny's jaw dropped. The house *hadn't* belonged to her grandfather's family. The "R" carved into the woodwork didn't stand for Richmond. It stood for Rose. Violet owned the house. Sunny had reached the end of the first document, and picked up the next to find Violet Rose Richmond's last will and testament, dated September 13, 1974. Her eyes darted through the pages until she found what she was looking for. In her will, which had been signed by Mr. Greenton, Violet had left the house and farmland to none other than Miss Maisy Edwards.

Just then Willow walked in the room. Sunny's heart was racing, trying to make sense of everything she had just read. Willow sat down with a sigh and said, "Oh Lord. I need a break." She looked tired, but far less angry than when they'd arrived home from Knoxville. She saw the papers scattered around the table. "What's all this?"

"It's the stuff from the safety deposit box. It's kind of incredible, mom."

"Oh yeah, I'm sure it's *real* thrilling."

"Hey, did mamaw have a will?"

"Nope. Daddy said she just wanted it all to go to him. I mean, she didn't own nothin' other'n her clothes and some whatnots." She added sarcastically, "And of course, all her precious flowers. Why?"

Sunny slid the documents across the table to her. "Actually, mom," she hesitated. "I think she owned everything. It's the *Rose* farm. Not the Richmond farm."

Without looking at the papers Willow responded with a scoff and said, "Now that's a bunch of bullshit. This farm was daddy's."

Sunny pointed to the paper tying the farm to the Rose family and gave her the long-story-short version of things. Then she pointed to Violet's will. "I really don't think it's bullshit, mom. To be honest I don't know what it is, but something's off. Something's not right with any of this."

Willow was silent as she looked at the papers. She began shaking her head and pushed the papers away, saying, "Nope. No. Not tonight. I can't deal with this right now. What are we gonna eat for supper? I ain't eatin' another frozen pizza."

Realizing she was fighting a useless battle, Sunny began putting the papers away. "I can drive into town and grab something, mom. You wanna come with?"

"Yeah, I'd like that, Sunny girl. Let me grab a drink first and then we'll hit the road." Willow didn't show it, but Sunny's discovery had shaken her to her core. Howard had always claimed the Richmond family built the home and farmed the land. Her mother never made such claims and never disputed his version of the story. Her instincts told her to shut it down, not dig any deeper, but a small part of her wanted the truth. Instead of listening to it, she decided to drown it in vodka.

Sitting at the small sandwich shop in town waiting for their food to arrive at the table, Sunny cautiously brought up what she knew was on both of their minds. She could only hope that it wouldn't set Willow off into a fit of insults toward Violet.

"I think we're going to have to find this Maisy person. Do you know who she is? Maybe she can explain what's going on with all that stuff from the bank or even the truth about the house." She looked at her mother, anticipating the worst possible reaction. To her surprise Willow remained calm.

"I don't know, Sun. I mean, the Edwards family owns the big farm next to ours. All that land, maybe 'bout fifty acres or more, belongs to them. The old man used to lease our land, and then when he died his son took it over. I don't remember the old man's wife's name. Maybe it was Maisy?" Willow sat quietly for a moment before continuing, "But this is all too much. It's like, kinda trippy, you know? I thought one thing all my life, and now you're saying it's all bass-ackwards. Maybe we just leave it be and not stir up any hornets' nests or anything. Besides, ol' Greenton said the house is mine."

Willow was scared, but she wasn't sure how to explain it. She didn't want to change her view of the world. There was a safety and familiarity she felt with the way she remembered everything about her childhood. She attended court-appointed therapy several years earlier and quickly learned that opening the door to the past was sure to bring out demons she had long forgotten about, and she intended to keep them forgotten. The sessions started out strong and somewhat beneficial, but the moment the therapist began asking about her parents Willow closed herself off and rode out the remainder of her appointments in near silence.

"But aren't you even a *little* bit curious? I mean, just the fact that it was *mamaw's* family home is so wild to me!" Sunny was excited. The secret key she found had indeed unlocked a treasure chest, but rather than money and jewels she found additional mysteries that she needed to solve. She hadn't yet considered the emotional toll this adventure could have on Willow.

"Yeah, I'll give you that. It's strange to think that it's actually mama's house. Fuckin' mind blowing is what it is. But to be honest, that makes me want to sell it even more. I don't *want* anything of hers." She paused as the waitress walked over with their plates. She smiled and thanked her before continuing. "I don't *need* anything of hers. Just like she didn't want or need me."

Sunny was silent for a moment, taken aback. She had never heard her mother say something so vulnerable. Willow was always venting her frustrations about Violet, but she never said anything about not being wanted. "Of course she wanted you, mom. She might have been strict with you and you all probably fought a lot, but that doesn't mean she didn't want you." The truth was, Sunny had no idea. She rarely saw her mother and her grandmother interacting. She was basing these statements solely on her own feelings as a mother. She couldn't imagine *not* wanting or needing Lilias.

Willow grinned. "Sweet, innocent, naive Sunny. You and I remember that woman *very* differently." She took a bite of her grilled cheese sandwich. "Goddamn. I forgot how good this place is. Remember comin' here when you's little?"

Sunny shook her head. "Not really. I mean, I know I've eaten here before but it wasn't memorable or anything."

"Really? Oh, you used to order a hotdog without a bun. They'd cut it up in little pieces for you with a toothpick stickin' outta each one. You thought you were hot shit eatin' so fancy like that." Willow smiled as she remembered her daughter being so little.

"That definitely sounds like some gourmet cuisine for sure." They continued talking for the rest of their meal, but never again mentioned Violet or the house. Sunny was glad her mom was stable, but she wondered how long it would last. Much like a volcano lying dormant for far too many years, Willow was due for an eruption at any moment.

As they drove home that evening, Sunny's mind drifted back to her grandmother and all the questions that now surrounded her. She couldn't understand how she'd gone her whole life without really knowing anything about her other than what Willow had told her. Her desire to learn more was no longer powered simply by the idea of an adventure or solving a mystery. Sunny wanted to know the truth so that she could tell Lilias about her roots beyond the apartments and trailer parks.

It was nearly two o'clock in the morning when Sunny came up with her plan. Her mind had been in turmoil for hours weighing pros and cons. She was due to fly back to New York the following evening, but leaving no longer felt like an option. The revelations she had uncovered about the farmhouse were too outrageous to ignore, and she couldn't help but feel like something was holding her here, urging her to dig deeper and find the answers. Ultimately, she needed to know that her mother was on board with her plan and she knew exactly how to make that happen.

The following morning Sunny decided to call Finley and tell him about her change of plans. As the phone trilled, her heart began beating harder and she began to get nervous.

"Hello, my love!" Finley answered. "We were hoping you'd call soon. Lil is here and dying to talk to you. We've had a big day so far." He passed the phone to their daughter before Sunny had a chance to even say hello to him.

"Mommy! Guess what! Guess what!" Lilias was squealing with excitement.

"Oh my goodness, Lil! What in the world is going on?"

"Granny and grandad bought me a fluffy cow! I named him Cookoo and he likes me and lets me pet him!"

"Oh boy! That's so great! You *definitely* need more stuffed animals taking up space on your bed," Sunny teased.

Lilias giggled. "Mommy! He can't fit in my bed! He sleeps in the barn, silly!"

Sunny paused. "Wait, Lil… Is Cookoo a *real* cow?"

Still giggling, she responded, "Of course he is! Are you coming today to see him? You can brush his hair!"

"Put daddy back on the phone, sweetie. Put daddy on the phone."

Lilias handed the phone back to Finley who was chuckling at his daughter's excitement. "Yeah?"

"*A fucking cow?!* They bought her a cow?! What happened to *not* spoiling her on this trip?" Sunny's nervousness had been replaced with anger. Finley's parents liked to buy Lilias anything her heart desired, despite Sunny's disapproval.

"Sun, it's not that big a deal. I'm sure they would've bought it anyway. They just had the back fields fenced in, so—"

"Oh my God. You've got to be kidding me. Stop enabling them! I don't want her growing up thinking she can just have whatever she wants whenever she wants it. It's one thing when it's Christmas or her birthday. But they do this shit all year long. We don't have enough room in our apartment for another toy let alone a goddamn cow."

"Feck's sake ye're in a mood. Spending a few days with yer maw and ye're starting to act more and more like her." The fact that he was back home with his family meant his accent was naturally thicker than normal. Knowing she was mad at him only made it worse. The only other times his accent would get stronger was if he'd had a few pints or he was angry. After a moment of silence, he asked, "So you head back to the city tonight, aye?"

Sunny took a deep breath. "That's what I wanted to talk to you about. Something's come up here, and I don't think I can leave yet." She braced for his response, but it was much harsher than she expected.

"Oh, this is jus' perfect. I shoulda known you'd do this. I mean, what am I supposed to tell Lil, huh? She's so anxious for you to get here and now you've decided you'd rather stay with yer bampot maw instead of spending the summer with your wean. *Real* nice, Sunny. Just top notch parenting."

"Jesus, Finn! First of all, speak English because you know I don't understand Scottish insults. Second, that's so unfair. I didn't *plan* on staying. I'd hoped to get out of here quickly, but there's a lot that I need to figure out. I mean, my grandfather left this house to my mom, but now I'm not even sure he owned it. There's no way my mom can do this on her own, so I need to—"

"You dinnae *need* to do anything. She's a grown woman, Sun. But this is what you do. You drop everything to take care of her as if she's a helpless wee child. She's not! She's just a shite adult, and ye're too blind to see it. She's using you like she always does, and —." Finn stopped himself before saying anything else hurtful.

"Wow. How long have you been holding *that* back?" Sunny's anger had returned. Normally she'd be apologetic and ask for his forgiveness, but this time felt different. This time she was staying for her own reasons and not because Willow had asked her to. "My mom doesn't even know I'm staying yet. I'm doing this for me and for Lil."

Finn laughed sarcastically. "Oh *really*?! Ye're doing this for *Lilias*? Avoiding her for the summer to hang out with your jakey maw?"

"I need to know about my family beyond the trailer parks, Finn! I don't have a castle to show her. I don't have the money to buy her cows and have park benches dedicated to her in a fancy garden near the Queen's estate. Your family is like a goddamn fairy tale and mine has always been more like a shameful secret that I'm embarrassed to even tell her. But now it seems like it was all a lie and I *need* to know the truth so that she can know who she is and where she comes from. She deserves that much. *I* deserve that much. It's important to me and that should make it important to you." Sunny was getting choked up, but she tried her hardest to hide that from him.

"Spending time with your daughter should be important to you," he snapped. "These are memories you'll never get back. She's only this young once. Just remember that."

Sunny's anger turned to rage. "How *dare* you, Finn? How dare you shame me like this?! You have no—"

"I'm not fighting with you about this anymore. I'll let you talk to Lilias and explain why ye're not coming." She could hear him pass the phone to their daughter.

"Are you coming today, mommy?!"

"Hey, Lil girl. I don't think I'm going to be able to come this time. I have a lot to work on here and help Mamaw Willy with some things. I'm sorry, love."

"Aww. That's not fair! Is it because Mamaw Willy is really sad 'cause her daddy died?"

"Sort of, but she's gonna be okay. And I really am very sorry I can't come be with you in Scotland. I'll keep calling you though so you can tell me all about your adventures."

"It's okay, mommy. I'll take a picture of Cookoo so you can see him though. He's the prettiest cow they had at the farm and they are going to bring him here tomorrow! I got to pick out a brush for him and I'm going to help feed him."

"That sounds like a good plan. Taking care of an animal like that is a big responsibility, so you be sure and work really hard, okay?"

"Okay, mommy. I love you!"

"I love you too, swee—"

"AND WATER!" Lilias loudly interrupted.

"What?"

"Cookoo needs water, too. Not just food. But it's for him to drink. Not like watering a plant." Lilias giggled at the thought of watering a cow.

Sunny chuckled. "You're such a silly girl. Have a great time and I'll talk to you soon." She hung up the phone relieved that Lilias wasn't upset with her, but the anger she felt toward Finley was only growing.

Willow had been waiting in the hallway. She'd heard Sunny arguing on the phone and knew something was going on. After waiting for a few moments in an effort to make it less obvious she had been eavesdropping, she walked in. "You alright?"

Sunny pulled back the covers to let Willow in the bed with her. "Finn's being a dick, that's all. Oh, and get this. His parents bought Lil a cow. *A real fucking cow!* Who does that?!"

"Oh no! They're making that sweet little girl happy! How could they possibly be such monsters?!" Willow began laughing. "Let 'em spoil her! Jesus! I wish I could buy her somethin' like that."

"Mom! No! I don't want her thinkin' she can have everything. It's not healthy."

Willow waved her off and said, "Nonsense. Ain't nothin' wrong with it as long as she knows *they* can have everything. *They* have the money. *They* buy all the things. Not everyone is like that. It's okay to let her know that some people have and some people don't have. Don't be mad at Finley just 'cause his mama and daddy got money to spend on her."

"Well, that's not the only reason I'm mad at him. I've actually been thinking, mom. With all this confusion about the house I decided I'm going to stay here for the summer. Is that okay with you?"

"*Is that okay with me?!* A whole summer with my Sunny girl?! Hell yes it's okay with me!" Willow hadn't felt this happy in years. She hugged her daughter close and felt some of her anxiety fade away. "I guess Finley weren't too happy about you stayin' here with me, huh?"

"Like I said, he's being a dick. He just doesn't understand. It'll be fine, mom."

"No, I know he don't like me after what happened and that's alright. I can't expect a rich boy like that to understand a hillbilly girl like me. While his mama was polishing her tiaras I's helpin' Toker make moonshine out in the woods."

"Oh God, I remember you tellin' me about him. You picked some winners, I'll give you that." Sunny chuckled thinking back to her mother's string of boyfriends.

Willow smiled. "Aw, Toker wasn't half bad. He was a good lay at least. Dumber'n a sack of rocks, bless his heart, but that never bothered me."

"Until that still blew up. I wonder if his eyebrows ever grew back in." They both began laughing.

Willow continued, "Lord, I never seen a man move so fast as when I hollered at him that his shirt was on fire. That man screamed and ripped off every stitch of clothing he had on and took off runnin' through the woods. And that's exactly how the sheriff found him. Naked as the day he's born. He tried hidin' in the bushes when he heard 'em yellin' for him, except he jumped right in a goddamn briar patch. That man couldn't catch a break that day." Sunny was laughing so hard she had tears in her eyes imagining the scenario playing out. After their laughter slowly faded out, Willow asked, "So what should we do today? Since you're here all summer, we can take a break from the house and go do somethin' fun. Or we can keep workin' here. Don't matter to me."

Sunny sat up. "Actually, mom, I think the most important thing is figuring out who really owns the house. If mamaw's will is valid then that means—"

"You're still on that? Mr. Greenton told me it was mine. End of story."

Sunny shook her head. "That's the problem. Mr. Greenton also signed mamaw's will. Maybe he can at least explain what is going on or who that Maisy woman is. The last thing we need is for her to show up and claim ownership." Sunny knew it was time to get her mother fully on board with her plan. "Because if she actually owns the house, then you get nothing."

Willow cocked her head to the side and was suddenly very agitated. "Oh hell no! We need to get that no-good Greenton on the phone right fuckin' now. I'll be damned if some stranger is gonna own *my* property. You heard him yesterday. *It's mine!*"

"That's a great idea, mom. We'll call him right now. Do you have his number?" As Willow quickly left the room to retrieve the lawyer's phone number, Sunny was delighted that her plan was falling into place just as she imagined it would.

"Here it is," Willow said as she walked back into the room waving a piece of notebook paper. "Here's his number. Get that bastard on the phone."

Sunny dialed and turned on the speaker phone. With each ring Willow cursed under her breath. Her anger was palpable, so Sunny motioned for her to calm down.

"Law Offices of William Greenton. This is Marie. How can I help you today?" answered Mr. Greenton's secretary.

Sunny replied, "Oh, hello. I am hoping to talk to Mr. Greenton about Howard Richmond's estate. I'm his granddaughter, Sunny. Mr. Greenton was here talking with us the other day and we just had a few questions about the will."

"Oh, certainly. Hold please."

After a short sample of an upbeat instrumental song, Mr. Greenton answered the call. "Hello, Sunny. How can I help you today?"

Without allowing Sunny a chance to talk, Willow shouted, "Why the fuck didn't you tell me my mama had a will, Greenton?!"

"*Mom! That's enough!*" Sunny scolded. "I'm so sorry. You see, we found this lock box at the bank in Knoxville and it contained my grandmother's will. We didn't know anything about it when she died, and not only does it look like she owned the farmhouse, but she left it to some woman named Maisy Edwards. And since you signed the will, we're hoping you can explain what is going on."

"I see," he responded. After taking a deep breath and collecting his thoughts he continued, "I'm afraid I can't be the one who— I mean, it's attorney-client privilege. I suggest reaching out to Ms. Edwards."

Willow's eyes grew wide but Sunny shushed her before she let him have it.

"I don't understand. How would we—" Sunny began asking before Mr. Greenton cut her off.

"My secretary can provide you with her address."

"Now listen here, Greenton, you son-of-a—" Before Willow could finish her insult, they were listening to the upbeat music again. "Did he hang up on me?" Sunny began to giggle. "He hung up on me! That motherfu—"

"Alright, I have that information for you ladies," Marie interrupted. "Do you have a pen and paper ready?" After speaking with the secretary and writing down the address, Sunny hung up the phone.

"What do you say, mom? Want to venture into the mountains to solve a mystery with me?" Sunny was smiling and half-pleading with her mother.

Willow sat silently for a moment, shaking her head and still angry. She simply wanted this all to be over with, but she couldn't resist appeasing her daughter's wishes. She sighed and while rolling her eyes answered, "Whatever."

Without saying a word, Sunny leaned over and hugged her mom. Despite feeling victorious for getting her way, she began to understand this experience was bound to be a rough emotional journey for Willow, and she was grateful that she wasn't putting up a fight...yet.

"As the crow flies, she don't live too far. But we gotta go into the mountains, so it might take a while," Willow said looking at an old map she found in the study.

"Why did you bring that ridiculously large map? I can just follow the GPS on my phone. God, get with the times, mom." Sunny was laughing at Willow as she tried to refold the creased, faded paper.

"I don't go places I'm not familiar with. If it ain't here or Knoxville, I don't have any business going." She gave up trying to fold it correctly and decided to frustratingly fold it her own way, shoving it in the glove compartment when she was done.

Sunny rolled her eyes and sighed. "I'm painfully aware of your geographical restrictions, mom. Look, it says we'll be there in like forty-five minutes."

Willow nervously watched the trees pass by the car window as they drove into the mountains. She could feel her anxiety rising with the elevation and she spent the car ride trying to decide what aspect of this trip was causing it—the fear of unknown places or stirring up memories of her mother. Obviously it was a combination of both, and the deeper they disappeared into the mountains the stronger her craving for a cigarette grew.

As the roads Sunny turned down began growing narrower and less maintained, Willow could no longer stay silent. "Are you sure that thing knows where it's going?" she asked, pointing to Sunny's cell phone.

"Yes, mom. It's fine. Trust me."

It was at that moment a loud voice from the phone announced, "Recalculating!"

Willow was startled and shouted, "Why's it doin' math?"

Sunny laughed. "We lost the cell signal for a second. It's fine. Good Lord. We really need to get you a new phone. Nobody uses a flip phone anymore, mom."

"Hey now! My phone does what it's supposed to do. It makes *phone calls*. I don't need it to take pictures or play music or whatever the hell else you do on that damn thing."

"You sound like you're eighty years old." Sunny looked back at her phone. "Oh shit. The signal is going in and out so much I don't know where to turn. *Shit!*" She pulled over to the side of the road and rolled down the window, holding her phone up into the sky.

Willow gave her a bewildered look, and opened up the glove compartment. She pulled out the incorrectly folded map, and after studying it for a few minutes she said, "Well, Sunny girl, looks like you're gonna want to turn left in about two miles. Then," she continued, tracing the road with her finger, "across a creek and I'd say about ten more miles we should start seeing some civilization. After that we just look at the house numbers." Sunny looked at the map, surprised at her mother's navigational skills. Willow sarcastically threw her hands up in the air while shouting, "Recalculating!"

"Oh shut up, mom," Sunny snapped as she began driving again.

It was nearly twenty minutes later that the car began slowing down in front of a cluster of homes on the side of the road. They didn't look to be anymore than shacks, and Sunny began to question whether this was a good idea or not. The thought of solving a mystery had seemed so exciting to her that she never considered it could be dangerous.

"I'm not seeing any mailboxes or house numbers, Sun. Anything over there on your side?" Willow had been looking through the passenger's side window at the rundown structures. Before she could answer, Willow rolled down her window while motioning for Sunny to stop. There was an old man sitting on a folding chair in front of one of the homes. He was wearing dirty overalls and an even dirtier hat. "Hey there, old timer! Beautiful day out, huh?"

He looked at Willow and nodded. Sunny was afraid of him, but she wasn't sure why. She figured it was because he was just sitting there, doing nothing. It seemed so strange to her after living in New York City for so many years and always seeing people coming and going but rarely sitting still. She checked that the doors were locked, despite the fact he looked like a strong wind might knock him clear off the chair.

"Say, we're lookin' for a Maisy Edwards. You reckon she lives 'round here?" Willow naturally had a country accent, but Sunny noticed she had turned it on extra thick while talking to this man. It was the same tactic she used when she worked as a waitress: a thicker accent almost always results in a bigger tip.

His frail, raspy voice said, "Yes'm. Miss Maisy live on over the hill." He pointed in the direction they were headed. "She got the home with the flowers. Can't miss it."

"Well thank you kindly, friend. You have a good one, alright?" Willow rolled up the window and smiled as the old man reached up and touched the tip of his hat. She turned back to Sunny and said, "Once again, no cell phone required."

As they drove over the hill Sunny wondered if they would know which home was Maisy's. The shacks all looked similar, like they were built by the same little shanty town architect, but the old man was right when he said they couldn't miss it. One shack was surrounded by a florist's paradise. It was a beautiful, organized chaos of perennials, annuals, decorative grasses, berry bushes, herbs, and even some vegetables. "Holy hell, mom. Look at this place!"

"That is a shitload of flowers, for sure. I'm guessing this woman is a downright loon. Bless her heart."

"That's the spirit, mom! Way to stay positive!" Sunny exclaimed sarcastically. "Let me do the talkin' okay? I don't need you going on a tear about mamaw right now. Just try to keep an open mind, yeah?"

"Ugh. Fine. I'll behave."

She opened the door, looked at the two women standing on her small wooden stoop, and before allowing them to speak she simply said, "Well, I guess this means you found the key. Either that or Greenton sent you." Maisy turned and walked back into her small home, leaving the door ajar for Sunny and Willow to follow. They looked at each other, not knowing what to say or what to expect next.

Maisy's home was no more than a living room area which doubled as her bedroom, a kitchen that consisted of a hot plate, sink, and icebox, and a small bathroom. To their surprise, the house was much nicer than they expected. Everything was neat and tidy and clean, much like Maisy herself. At just over one hundred pounds, she was a very petite woman in her mid-seventies dressed in a plain cotton tee-shirt and a long skirt. She was far too young to be the wife of old man Edwards as Willow had predicted. Sunny and Willow moved across the room silently as Maisy motioned toward the couch for her guests to take a seat.

Sunny spoke first, as was the plan. "So you're Maisy Edwards, huh?"

"You guessed right, little Sunflower." She put a tea kettle on the hot plate and set out three tea cups. Looking past Sunny, she spoke in a cautious tone, "Willow."

Willow was thrown off guard. She looked at Sunny and then back at Maisy. "Uhh, yeah. Hey. I mean, hi, Maisy—err, Miss—umm, ma'am." Maisy had turned back to the tea kettle. Willow looked to Sunny again and shrugged.

"Let me finish preparing the tea and then I'll tell you whatever you would like to know." Sunny noticed Maisy's accent was mild and her speech was far more eloquent than most of the mountain folk she'd met in her life.

While they waited, Sunny and Willow looked around the house from their seats on the couch. There weren't a lot of decorations besides flowers, both alive and dried. It was minimal, yet tasteful. On the end table next to Sunny was a small black and white photograph of a young Violet. She nudged her mother and pointed it out, wondering why her grandmother's photo seemed to be the only one in the house. Willow shrugged again but was more animated in an effort to remind Sunny she had no idea who this woman was or how her mother played into all of this.

Maisy poured the tea, handed each of her guests a cup and saucer, and joined them by sitting in the armchair with her own cup of tea. "Well now, what sort of questions do you have for me?"

They looked at each other and before Sunny could answer, Willow went ahead and started things off. "Who the hell are you?" Sunny's eyes became wide and her lips became tight as she silently scolded her mother.

To their relief, Maisy simply laughed. "I was dear friends with your mother, Willow. That's who the hell I am. I grew up on the farm next door to you all."

"I'm sorry, but I never knew my mama to have any friends."

"We grew up together from about the time we were four or five years old. I first met her when my daddy started working the land for Miss Cora, Violet's mother. That would be your grandmother, Willow. And Sunny, well she'd be your great-grandmother. Violet and I were best friends all through school, and Miss Cora, she'd let me come over to visit whenever I wanted. I practically lived there at the farm most of my childhood. I always thought it was a castle with Cora as the queen and me and Vi as the princesses." She looked at the small framed photograph of Violet and smiled.

Sunny was also smiling while listening to Maisy talk, but Willow was less sentimental. "So if you two were so close, how come I never even *heard* of you? I don't remember a girl living on the Edwards farm."

Maisy took a sip of her tea and sat back in her chair. She knew Willow was close with Howard, and she wanted to avoid speaking too harshly. "I moved out of my mama and daddy's house when you were still a little baby, Willow. I've been living up here in the mountains ever since. Besides, I was no longer allowed at the farmhouse." There was so much more she wanted to say. So much more that *needed* to be said, but it had to be laid out delicately.

"So how do you know about us?" Sunny asked.

"Violet would show me pictures of you when we'd meet. Of course I haven't seen either of you in a few years since she passed, but you mostly look the same." Maisy seemed so feeble, yet somehow strong at the same time.

"I noticed in the letters that were in the safety deposit box that you talked a lot about flowers with my mamaw. Did you teach her how to be a gardener or did she—" Sunny had tried to get a question in, but Willow cut her off.

"What do you mean '*no longer allowed*'? My mama get a restraining order against you or somethin'?"

"Once Vi and Howard were married I was no longer welcome at the house. Your mother became pregnant and devoted her life to being a homemaker and taking care of her family." It was taking all of Maisy's strength to not give them every detail from the past.

"So you two just fell out of touch?" Willow seemed to ask the question to nobody in particular. She then turned to Sunny and asked, "Then why the hell did she leave *her* the house? Why wouldn't it go to daddy? You know what I'm thinking?" Sunny began trying to calm her mother down to no avail. "I think this ol' bag is trying to get the house so she can move out of this shack in the mountains. Yeah, you heard that my daddy died and you're hoping to cash in."

Maisy remained calm despite Willow's verbal aggression. "No, dear. I can assure you that is not what's happening. After my father passed, my brother, Archie, took over our farm. He leased your farmland from Howard for many years. I'm sure you remember that. In all honesty, it was more like one big farm than two separate family farms. I always assumed that's why Vi left things to me in her will. And your mother and I *never* fell out of touch. We simply had to keep our friendship a secret."

Willow was silent but visibly annoyed while Sunny took the bait. "Why a secret?"

Maisy took a moment before answering, choosing her words carefully. "Howard Richmond did not want us to remain friends. I was banned from the farmhouse and she was forbidden from visiting me at my home. Howard was... not a kind man."

"Bullshit! He was a *great* man. How would you even know? You weren't ever around him!"

"Okay, take it easy, mom." Sunny turned back to Maisy and said, "I'm sorry, but that really *doesn't* sound like my grampa."

Maisy nodded. "You're right. You never saw the side of him that I knew. The side that Violet knew. He had quite a jealous streak in him. That's why we could only meet up in private. He never liked that we were so close. So we'd sneak around to try and spend time together. It was tough at first because he was always suspicious, and once the baby was born," she said, motioning to Willow, "well, it got even harder. But once you started to grow up, we figured out more ways to see each other. She had more excuses for leaving the house at that point. Then we thought up the gardening club idea." She chuckled at this. "Howard had no interest in flowers, but he let her take up gardening. Whenever I'd see her I'd send her home with new types of flowers for her to plant, that way he'd think she'd really been to a nursery or flower shop. Pretty soon she had a magnificent flower garden to be proud of. She said she even caught Howard admiring it at one point."

Sunny smiled. "She loved that garden. I used to spend time out there with her. She always seemed happiest when she was there."

"Every flower I gave her had purpose. You see, my grandmother studied the language of flowers, and that's how I learned it." She pointed to a vase on a small shelf near the door. "See that?"

"You mean those weeds?" Willow asked bitingly, still seething from the unkind words about her father.

"Lots of people think it's weeds, but it's actually called Queen Anne's Lace. I always try to have some there, because they mean security and sanctuary. Having them there helps me feel safe in my home."

Sunny looked confused. "I thought those were, like, really poisonous."

Maisy shook her head. "No, dear. You're thinking of hemlock. They look very similar, but I can tell the difference. Now don't you go trying to pick some Queen Anne's Lace if you see it. You don't know the difference, and hemlock can kill a person if you aren't careful."

Willow was growing impatient with the conversation. She looked at Sunny and asked, "I'm sorry, but did we come here for a gardening lesson?"

Sunny rolled her eyes, and looked back to Maisy. "Okay, so you two stayed friends all that time, but my grampa never knew?"

Maisy nodded. "It was a miracle that he didn't. Even as we grew into old ladies, we had to keep it all a secret."

"This is so wild. I mean, I don't understand why he wouldn't be okay with it or why she wouldn't just be friends with whoever she wanted." Sunny was hoping to maintain control of the conversation so that Willow didn't lose her temper again.

"It's a very complicated matter. I'm not sure you're ready for the whole story today." Maisy sat her empty teacup on the coffee table. "The fact is Howard was very controlling, and Violet was terrified of him. She didn't dare stand up to him or openly defy him."

Willow scoffed. She stood up and walked to the door, which only took her three or four steps in a house that small. She looked at Sunny and snapped, "I'm not listening to this anymore. I'll be in the car." She slammed the door behind her.

"I'm so sorry, Miss Maisy. She's still just so upset about his death, and she's always had this complicated relationship with my mamaw. I should really—"

"You mustn't let her shut down," Maisy leaned forward and grabbed Sunny's arm. "She can't quit now. You brought her this far. She *needs* to know the truth. You both deserve the truth." Sunny was shaken by the intensity in which Maisy was speaking and the fire in her eyes. Maisy then reached over to the end table where Violet's photo was displayed. She opened the drawer and pulled out another letter and handed it to Sunny. "Take this. It will help you understand. Bring her back and I can make her see."

Sunny took the letter and walked to the door. "I'll do my best, but I can't promise anything when she's like this. She'll need to cool off for a while. Can I get your phone number so that I can call and let you know when we'll come back?"

Maisy looked around at her small, simple home. "What makes you think any of us up here has a phone?" she asked candidly.

"Right. Sorry. We'll be back, um, at some point. Thanks for your time today, and again I'm sorry for her outbursts. Please don't take it personally. It's just the way she—"

"Christ almighty, you apologize too much. I'm far too old to get offended. Now go on. Get out of here before it gets dark and you lose your way home."

Back at the farmhouse that evening, Sunny sat at the table with the letter Maisy had given her. Willow had started to work on clearing out her father's bedroom again as a way to destress from their visit into the mountains. Her anxiety had increased more than she had anticipated, and she was unsure of how to control her emotions surrounding all the new information she and Sunny were learning. Willow didn't know about the new letter, and Sunny wasn't going to mention it until she knew what it said. Something told her whatever Maisy knew was going to change everything. She still wasn't convinced that her grandfather was as awful as Maisy claimed, and with her mother already teetering on the edge of a breakdown, Sunny had to proceed with caution. If she could unravel this mystery on her own, she could figure out a way to explain it to Willow without completely unraveling her world as well.

She opened the envelope, which had been addressed to her grandmother at the P.O. box, to find that it wasn't actually a letter at all. It was more like a list of definitions. Sunny began studying the two handwritten columns:

Floriography

Anemone - Forsaken love	Lavender - Distrust
Basil - Hate	Oak - Strength, bravery
Camellia - Longing	Orchid - Beauty
Dandelion - Fortune-telling	Roses - Love
Dogwood - Love over adversity	Snowdrop - Hope
Fern - Secrecy, magic	Thistle - Hate and distrust
Heather - Protection	Rosemary - Remembrance

Sunny read through the entire page full of flowers and their meanings. She sat for a few moments feeling frustrated. Knowing she had to get more information, Sunny decided a second meeting was in order.

The next morning, Sunny woke up early and left a note for Willow on the kitchen table. She claimed she was headed into Knoxville for a few hours because of a work email she received. Willow had never really understood or even cared to understand what her daughter's job as a writer entailed, so her reason was vague enough to be believable and not lead to further questions or the need for additional explanations. Sunny got in her rental car and headed back into the mountains.

Maisy was pulling weeds in front of the house when Sunny arrived. Her garden smock was dirty, so she took it off and hung it near the front door. They sat on wooden chairs in the garden amongst the flowers while they talked. Sunny couldn't help but think back to sitting in her grandmother's garden as a child, and she suddenly missed her deeply.

"So does it all make sense yet?" Maisy asked, fanning herself with a newspaper that had been sitting in one of the chairs.

"What? No! If anything I have even more questions now." Sunny was scrambling to understand what she might have missed.

Maisy chuckled. "Okay. What would you like to know? And where's your mother? I told you she needs to be here to learn the truth as well."

Sunny shook her head. "No, not yet. I need to know what's going on before her. You don't know her like I do. She could very well lose her ever-lovin' mind over this. If I understand it, I can explain it to her in a way that hopefully keeps her sanity intact."

"Very well then. Ask me your questions."

"Well, umm, I guess first I'd like to know how that list of flowers was supposed to help me. I mean, it's interesting but how in the hell would I make sense of anything based on that?"

Maisy rolled her eyes and sighed. "A detective you are not. I told you my grandmother studied flower meanings. I copied that list out of an old book she had. I knew if Howard should ever find one of the letters, he'd be none the wiser of what was truly being said." Maisy was smiling at the thought of her trickery.

Sunny thought about that for a few seconds before her eyes got wide and she excitedly whispered, "*It's a code! Oh my God, you wrote to my mamaw in code!*"

Laughing, Maisy replied, "There it is! I knew you'd get there eventually."

Sunny sat up a little straighter in her chair, speaking a bit faster. "Okay, so now I'm thinking you used a post office box to make sure my grampa never got to the letters first?"

Maisy nodded. "That's exactly right. I told you he had a jealous streak in him. Oh, it was an awful situation. I knew Violet was in danger with that man, so that's when we set up that mailbox as a way to keep in touch."

Sunny sat there, stunned. "*Danger?* That seems a bit extreme—"

Paying no attention to Sunny's statement, Maisy continued, "First thing I did was send her the flower meanings. I'd taught her about them before, and even Miss Cora liked to learn about it. She loved the idea that she'd named her daughter Violet, which means modesty. It fit her so well. Vi never wanted anyone to fuss over her and always put others first. And Cora was delighted when she learned that Violet was expecting a baby. She suggested naming the baby after a flower and making it a new family tradition."

"Wait, what?! I never knew where that came from!"

"Yes, that's it. It's from your great-grandmother Cora." Maisy smiled seeing that Sunny was genuinely interested in this historical fact about her family.

"Okay, so what does Willow mean?"

"Grief."

"Oh shit," Sunny responded. "Sorry, it's just that, you know, that's pretty messed up."

"Violet was in a deep depression at that time. It wasn't *because* of the baby, quite the opposite actually. Willow was truly the only bit of joy in her life. Willows have several meanings. One is grief and mourning, but another has to do with the strength we gain from weathering fierce storms."

"No matter how it was meant my mother will definitely take it as a personal insult. How about Sunflower?" Once again, she couldn't say her own name without a hint of contempt in her voice. "What does my name mean?"

"Sunflowers are symbolic of an intense love."

"Really?" Sunny grinned thinking of her mother naming her something so profound despite only being a child herself.

"In the spirit of keeping things honest, Willow had no idea what it meant. She had it in her mind that she was a hippie back then.

Luckily Violet forbade her from naming you 'Flower Power Richmond'. So just know that it could have been worse."

"Good Lord," Sunny said as she scrunched her face in disgust, causing Maisy to laugh even harder. "Alright, my daughter's name is Lilias which is the Scottish version of Lily. Do I even want to know what the meaning is?"

"Purity and innocence, my dear. Truly the perfect name for a child." Maisy smiled and looked toward a group of lilies planted in her garden.

"Oh thank God. That could have made for an awkward conversation in the future." After a few moments of silence as the women looked around the colorful garden, full of buzzing from the many honeybees, Sunny finally spoke. "Why would you say that my mamaw was in danger with my grampa?"

Maisy nodded. "He was a very powerful man in this town, even at a young age when they were first going together. After a while, he didn't like the idea of her spending time with anyone but him. He convinced her that she wasn't worthy of love or friendship. Wouldn't even let her get a job. In public he was very personable with everyone, but at home he was very different indeed."

"I don't know. I lived with them for a long time and I never noticed him being—"

Maisy cut her off. "By then they were mostly separated. She moved into her own bedroom around the time you were born. He didn't put up much fuss about it. As long as she kept the house clean, put food on the table, and took care of you and your mama he left her alone most of the time."

"But why wouldn't she just leave him if he was that awful?"

"I told you. She was terrified of him! I know he threatened her more than once. He couldn't stand the idea of what people might think of him, *the mayor*, having a wife that left him. He was just an awful man to her. I'm sorry for talking poorly of someone you cared for, but personally I'm happy he's dead."

"Jesus Christ. This is a lot to take in." Sunny was rubbing her forehead, unsure how to process this information. "I think I'm gonna need a few days to think this through. And you're right that my mom probably needs to hear this, but I don't think she'll handle it very well at all."

"Bring her to me. You don't have to tell her anything you don't feel comfortable talking to her about. I will *show* her the truth. Your job is to simply get her here." The intensity had returned to her voice, and Sunny knew she was serious.

"Yes, ma'am. I'll make sure she comes back. I promise."

As she got up from her chair and began to walk toward her house she said, "You, too, will come to know the whole story."

"Wait, what? I thought you just told me the whole story."

Maisy didn't respond. She merely laughed as she disappeared into her home, leaving Sunny alone with her thoughts and the honeybees.

"You get everything sorted out for work, Sunny girl?" Willow was sitting on a rocking chair on the wrap-around porch drinking lemonade.

"Hey, mom. Yeah, it's all worked out. Just needed to go somewhere with a better internet connection, you know?" Sunny sat on the other rocking chair next to her mother.

"Oh for God's sake, did I not teach you to lie any better'n that?"

Sunny's heart sank into her stomach. "What do you mean? I'm not lying about anything."

"Oh really? They got a good connection up there in the mountains? Ol' Maisy got an internet cafe set up back behind the shack?" Willow shook her head. "You ought to be ashamed. Can't tell a lie to save your life."

"Why would I ever want to lie to you?" She knew she'd been caught, but for some reason she couldn't give in yet.

"Because you're a daughter and I'm your mama! It's what you're supposed to do! Hell, I lied to your mamaw all the time. Ugh. Remind me to teach you how to lie before you go back to New York. How do you survive without bein' able to tell a damn lie?" She took a sip of her lemonade and looked out over the fields. "So, pray tell, what did Miss Maisy have to say today?"

Sunny sighed and slumped back in her chair. "Just that you should really come back and talk to her some more. She really does know some interesting things about our family history that I think you'd like to know."

Willow had been shaking her head the entire time Sunny was speaking. "Why? What good does it do me? Ain't gonna change anything. She could tell me my mama was a goddamn saint, but it don't fix how she treated me. And if she wants to sit there and talk shit about daddy, well then screw that. I ain't hearin' it."

Sunny was outwardly frustrated this time. "Ugh! You *never* have an open mind about anything! How can you *not* want to know about your family and what they were like before you were even here?! It's killing me to not understand all this. I mean, who were they? Why all the secrets? I've basically got whiplash now from this trip after finding out they not only lived in separate rooms but that they didn't even get along. That maybe he was mean to her and maybe she was miserable. And you don't seem to care at all. I just don't get it, mom. I don't get it." Sunny was shaking her head and trying to keep from tearing up. She hadn't expected to react so passionately.

Willow stood up and sneered, "If you don't get it by now, you obviously ain't been listenin' to me your whole life." With that she headed back into the house. Sunny realized getting her mother to revisit Maisy would prove to be more challenging than she had anticipated. It briefly crossed her mind that if she got her drunk enough she might be able to trick her into going, but she hated to take it that far.

Sunny walked across the driveway toward the old milking barn. The garden Violet had been so proud of had been overgrown for several years. Large antique wagon wheels still framed the garden entrance. Just as she had always done as a child, she walked between them and down what had been the center aisle of the garden that led to Violet's favorite spot. She cleared off a bit of English ivy that had taken hold of the bench and sat down. Trying her hardest to remember what flowers were planted, Sunny wished she had paid more attention to all the things her grandmother had told her back then. She longed to hear her voice one more time. She begged her brain to conjure up the long lost images of how it all used to look, but she couldn't see past the weeds. She wished she could bring Lilias to Tennessee and show her the garden as it was so many years ago, simply to see the wonder in her eyes. It wasn't fair that the most magical parts of Sunny's childhood were disappearing before she could ever share them with her own daughter.

Sunny knew she needed to figure out how her mother would react to everything she had just learned from Maisy. Her own mind was still spinning between total disbelief and complete shock. It was not unlike her mental state after the one and only car wreck she was involved in. One minute she understood her life and knew exactly where she was and the next she found herself upside-down in a ditch unsure of what to do next. She didn't want to believe what Maisy had said about her grandfather because she had always looked up to him as a respectable man, but her thoughts were tormented by the possibility that her grandmother had been mistreated by him. Despite never noticing any physical or verbal abuse between her grandparents, Sunny *had* witnessed all types of abuse directed at her mother from various boyfriends and husbands over the years.

Willow's disastrous relationships started in high school. Toker, the moonshine still detonator, wasn't so much abusive as he was negligent and reckless. Willow needed someone to support her emotionally, but instead he would simply give her drugs as a way to show affection. She became friends with Toker in summer school after she gave birth to Sunny in 1973. Never revealing the identity of Sunny's father, Willow started running with a new set of friends that didn't judge her for her poor decisions. Her old friends, the cheerleaders and football players, no longer wanted to associate with someone so flawed, and the parents of those kids had encouraged keeping her as an outcast so as to not poison the rest of the group. Willow often hoped that two of those parents would have taken a good look at Sunny's face, because they would have seen several features from their own child staring back at them. Toker's friends, on the other hand, had no problem with flawed people and loved to smoke pot and take recreational drugs, neither of which Willow had ever tried before. In an effort to blend in with her new friends, she shared a bottle of Quaaludes with them that had been prescribed to her during a postpartum checkup where she complained of insomnia. The doctor had taken pity on her, but the moment Violet saw the pills she refused to let her have any. Violet was adamant that Willow take responsibility for the new baby she brought into the world, and that would include many sleepless nights, whether she liked it or not.

Once she felt the effects of the pills she was hooked. She craved that feeling all day and all night. Occasionally she would smoke pot or get drunk, but she preferred the pills because there was no scent left on her clothing, no alcohol on her breath, and no real hangover the next day. Toker was an on and off love interest of Willow's for several years. Sunny was too young to really remember much about him aside from the fact that he seemed like a goofy kid. Once he was arrested after the still explosion, Willow decided it was time to move on for good.

Her first husband, Jimmy, was bad news from the day they met. They were married after knowing each other for two months and Willow moved in with him, bringing Sunny along for the ride. This was Sunny's first home away from the farmhouse, and she truly thought they would be a family. She was still quite young, only four years old, but she remembered the trailer was filthy and there was always a cloud of smoke clinging to the ceiling of each faux-wood paneled room. She could still clearly see the strip of sticky paper covered in dead flies hanging over the table where she would eat her meals. Sunny quickly learned to keep her mouth shut and stay out of Jimmy's way. He never struck her, but Willow was not so lucky. Jimmy would regularly shove her or smack her or grip her arm so tightly it would send her to her knees in pain. Willow gave as good as she got, causing him black eyes, cigarette burns, and four stitches from a beer bottle to the head. Sunny would simply go to her room when the shouting started, because she knew the violence would come next. One day after a particularly rough fight, a neighbor called the police to report a domestic situation in the trailer park. Seeing the environment they were living in, Child Protective Services were also called in and Sunny was removed from the home. Howard quickly called Mr. Greenton to ensure she was placed back at the farmhouse where she stayed for the next several years.

During the time Sunny was back with her grandparents, Willow divorced Jimmy and went through a string of failed relationships. Most of the men were dealers she simply used as a way to support her addiction. Quaaludes were still her drug of choice, and in their small town there seemed to be an endless supply of prescriptions being handed out. Sunny rarely saw her mother during this period. Usually she'd stop by the house once or twice a week to ask for money, but there never seemed to be time for bonding between mother and daughter. Consequently, Sunny relied on Violet to be more of a mother than a grandmother, making it much harder for her to leave again when she was twelve.

When she moved into the new trailer with Willow, things appeared stable at first. The house was clean, the air was smokeless, and there were no dead fly chandeliers hanging over the table. Sunny felt safe with her mother for once, and she was truly enjoying it. She missed being with her grandparents, but they were only a few miles away and Willow would always make sure Sunday dinners were spent together as a family at the farm. Assuring everyone that she was off the pills, Willow seemed to have her life in order. That's when she met Brian, a man who had a good job. A man who was smart and told corny jokes to try and make Sunny laugh. A man who treated Willow with respect and kindness. They were married just after Sunny's thirteenth birthday. Everything seemed perfect in their new little family until Willow's first breakdown tore it all apart.

Blinded by love and his desire for a picture-perfect family, Brian began enabling Willow's drug habit in order to keep the peace. At first, she continued functioning quite well and nobody else in the family suspected anything was amiss. Willow was working as a waitress during that time. She began requesting to be put on the late shifts and wouldn't arrive home until the early hours of the morning the following day, despite the restaurant having closed well before midnight. Willow would then sleep most of the day, becoming increasingly belligerent anytime she was disturbed. Sunny knew something was going on, but she never wanted to upset her mother so she pretended as if everything was okay. The night it all came to a head was burned into her memory like an inescapable nightmare.

One evening in 1988, Brian decided it would be a fun surprise to have dinner at the restaurant since Willow was always working the evening shift and they'd not had a family meal together in months. Upon arriving at the restaurant and not seeing her anywhere, the hostess informed them that Willow had actually been fired a few weeks before. Brian was hurt by her deception but also worried for her safety. Not knowing where his drug addicted wife might be, he played it off as no big deal so as to not upset Sunny and cause her to panic. The fact was, Sunny wasn't upset or panicked. She was angry, and she had a good idea of where her mom might be. Providing directions to an abandoned ranger station in the mountains, Sunny led her stepfather right to her mother's location. She'd been with Willow to pick up drugs at that house so many times it was easy for her to remember the way. Loud music could be heard from the overgrown dirt parking area and smoke was rolling out of the windows. As they entered a room lit only with a blacklight and a strobe light, they saw four men standing around smoking joints and throwing darts, two women snorting lines of cocaine off of a small makeup mirror, and in the corner was Willow, performing oral sex on her drug dealer. Willow was in the midst of a high that Sunny had never witnessed before that night, and she fooled herself into believing that it must have been the first time her mother had tried the new fad known as "crack". Seeing the rage in her eyes when she noticed Brian standing in the doorway and then watching her physically attack him before two of the other men in the room were able to pull her off was a terror Sunny had never known before or since. Once separated Willow began to sob uncontrollably, begging Brian to forgive her. Sunny helped him get her in the car, and the only sound as they drove was the hum of the tires on the road. After they arrived back home that evening, Brian put Willow in bed and began packing his bags. By morning, he and all his belongings were gone. Sunny couldn't help but feel responsible since the catalyst that triggered the entire chain of events was none other than her fifteenth birthday dinner. Sunny moved back to the farmhouse, and neither Willow nor Sunny had ever spoken of that night since.

Unlike all the failed relationships she had encountered with men, Willow always saw her father as good, honest, and hard-working. Sunny knew hearing something so damning would break her. So far Willow had been able to put herself back together after tragedies, but this sort of news would shatter her. Sunny feared there would be no coming back from something this life-altering. Perhaps it *was* best for Maisy to tell her. If Sunny did it herself, Willow might shut down before agreeing to go see Maisy again. She began formulating the conversation in her mind as she walked back to the house.

Sunny and Willow continued cleaning out the house for the next week. There was no mention of Maisy or the contents of the safety deposit box. They made several trips to the dump and the Hope House, a local charity that collected household items for people in need. Real progress was being made, and both women felt a sense of accomplishment as they walked through the mostly empty bedrooms. Things were going well, but Sunny knew it was time to have the first of what she knew would be many arduous conversations.

Crawling into bed with Willow before she had fallen asleep, Sunny snuggled up next to her. Willow reached over, turned on the bedside lamp, and sat up asking, "Okay, Sunny girl. What do you want?"

"*Want?!* Why do I have to want something? I just thought it would be nice to—" Willow looked at her with raised eyebrows. "Okay, fine." Sunny sat up on the bed across from her mother, hugging the blanket just as she would do when she was little and nervous to ask for something. "I want you to come with me to see Maisy again."

"Oh come on. You're still on this? I thought we'd moved past it."

"Nope. Maybe you're done, but I'm definitely not done, mom. The mystery of it all is killing me inside. I don't know how you're so indifferent about it. And to be honest, that's driving me just as crazy as everything else." Sunny was delighted that her mother hadn't instantly shut down or started screaming.

"I just don't see why it matters. I own the house now, so—"

"But do you?" Sunny interrupted. "Because mamaw had a will, and in it she left the house to Maisy. As far as I can tell, grampa didn't actually *own* the house. And if he was lying about that, maybe he lied about other things." She wished she'd not said that last part, but it was too late. It had already been released into the room.

To Sunny's surprise, Willow responded completely out of character. "You know, that's the part that's been botherin' me, too. Daddy would always brag about this being *his* family's home. But why wouldn't mama speak up? Why wouldn't she set him straight?"

"You really need to talk to Maisy, mom. I think she knows a lot more than we realize. Maybe that was the only thing he lied about, and he was perfect otherwise. But I'd really like to know why he lied about the house, if nothing else."

"Why do you care? I mean, how does this change things for you? It's like you're lookin' for a juicy piece of gossip about two people who are dead and in the ground. I don't see how it's relevant to—"

"For Lilias, mom! I want her to know where she comes from, and I don't want it to be based on lies and fairy tales. Since you refuse to tell me who my father is then grampa and mamaw are all I have. But if I'm telling Lil that mamaw was an amazing woman and you're telling her that she was awful, she'll never know the truth. Right now we have a chance to really learn about her from someone who knew her before either of us existed. Aren't you even the least bit curious as to why she was the way she was?" Suddenly Sunny was the irate one and Willow was staying calm. It was a dynamic neither of them was used to.

"I do want to know, Sun. I'm just, I don't know how to describe it. Scared, I guess. I'm scared to hear what she might say. If daddy lied I have to believe he had a good reason to. But what if he wasn't a good man like I always thought? I just don't know how to deal with that." Willow was still outwardly resisting, but the truth was that she had been thinking about her mother owning the house all week. It kept her up at night. The more she wrestled with it the more she wanted answers.

"We'll deal with it together, mom. It's going to affect me, too. I always thought grampa was such a brilliant and kind man. But I have to know the truth. I have to, for Lil."

Willow sat silently, looking out her bedroom window at the old milking barn. There was a light just over the barndoor that illuminated Violet's old garden. Finally Willow said, "You know, Sun, you're a shitty liar. But I'll be damned if you don't always get your way." She paused for a moment as Sunny looked at her with the anticipation of a child. Willow sighed and said, "Fuck it. Take me back up the mountain." Sunny squealed with glee and tackled her mom back onto the bed, causing her to shout, "Goddammit, Sunny! You're bound to kill me actin' like a lunatic. Now go to your own bed!"

Sunny couldn't stop smiling as she left the room that night, prancing with giddiness. They had no idea how extraordinarily their lives were going to forever change on that mountain.

Arriving at Maisy's house up in the mountains, Sunny noticed Willow began wringing her hands. With no cigarettes or alcohol nearby she hoped the anxiety wouldn't be too much. Unbeknownst to her, Willow was thinking the same thing. She felt the slightest bit of shame for how she acted during their first visit, so this time her inner dialogue had been focused on being open-minded and less combative. If nothing else, she wanted to make Sunny happy.

A few moments after knocking on the door, Maisy opened it and was pleasantly surprised to see both women there. "Oh, you made it! You *both* made it! Well, this is just wonderful. You stay right there and I'll get my sweater." And then she closed the door. Willow and Sunny looked at each other and shrugged before Maisy opened the door again and walked out past them. She shouted over her shoulder, "Come on! No time to waste. Just a short walk through the woods." Sunny began to follow her, hesitantly.

"*We're hiking?!*" Willow acted appalled.

"Mom, I have no idea what is happening but she's obviously not stopping." Sunny walked quickly to try and catch up with Maisy. Willow stayed a comfortable distance behind them.

The morning's rain had left everything damp and somewhat muddy along the trail. It was nearly a ten minute walk on the winding path surrounded by overgrown woods, but eventually Sunny could see a shack up ahead. She noticed there were a lot of ferns and dandelions growing the closer they got to it, and she wondered if that was a coincidence or if those had been planted purposefully. Sunny never would have given them a second thought before, but with Maisy's secret flower codes she was determined to remain vigilant and piece things together. Despite the shack being similar in size to Maisy's, it was in considerably worse shape. The roof was damaged from years of storms, one of the windows was busted, and it looked like a rodent might have chewed through the makeshift foundation.

Maisy slowed down and waited for Willow to catch up. Once she reached them, she put her hands on her hips and looked at the shack. "Are you fixin' to murder us, Maisy? Because if it means that much to you, you can have the house."

"I'm not going to kill you, Willow. I just want to introduce you to someone."

Sunny looked back at the shack. "Wait... Someone *lives* in there?!"

Maisy chuckled and said, "You've lived in the big city too long. Yes, as a matter of fact my aunt lives here. She's really quite old but sharp as a tack. She might ramble on once she starts talking, but I do have a reason for bringing you here. I promise."

It was dim inside the shack, as the windows were shrouded by makeshift curtains. Once their eyes had adjusted from being in the sunlight, Sunny and Willow could see some very meager furnishings filling the single room. A sink with a constant, monotonous drip sat in the corner. There was a cot with a raggedy blanket and pillow along the far wall. A large wooden table filled nearly half the room, and behind that was a fireplace with flames rising up around a large cast iron pot. Next to the fire was a remarkably old woman in a rocking chair, using her ornately carved cane to rock herself back and forth.

Willow grabbed Sunny's arm and gasped.

Startled, Sunny looked around the room quickly, clinging to her mother and asked,"Mom, what the hell?"

Willow's gaze was fixed on the old woman as she whispered, *"Cemetery goblin!"* Sunny didn't understand at first, but then it hit her. It was the ominous woman they met after Howard's funeral.

"Aunt Theora! I brought you some company!" shouted Maisy.

Theora looked toward Willow and Sunny and said, "I don't know why she yells. I hear her perfectly fine." She spoke slowly in a peculiar accent. "No sense in standing around all day. You may sit, if you please." Maisy took the chair closest to Theora while Sunny pulled two chairs out from the table for her and Willow.

"Willow, Sunny, this is my Aunt Theora. She is my mother's sister," Maisy said. "Willow, I know you don't want to hear what I have to say about your father. That's where Theora can help."

"I'm sorry, but I don't know that I want to hear what she has to say about him either," Willow replied.

Theora spoke up, saying, "I never met the man."

Willow looked at Maisy while gesturing to Theora, "Oh yeah, she's gonna be a big help."

"Settle down. She's not going to *tell* you about him. You see, Theora is a bit of a, umm, chemist."

Willow couldn't hold back her laughter. Sunny smacked her arm and whispered sharply, "Mom! Stop it!" She didn't show it, but Sunny was biting the inside of her cheek to keep from laughing as well.

"I'm sorry, but a *chemist?!* You can't blame me for this. I mean, you've got to be kidding, right?"

Maisy was serious. Neither she nor Theora was laughing. "Most people around these mountains know her as a witch, but the truth is she was professionally trained in creating potions for medicinal purposes."

Willow was shaking her head, still chuckling. "Hell's bells. You know, I'm just tryin' to wrap my head around this real quick. I feel fine. Why would you bring me to a witch doctor? Alls I need to know is what the deal is with my damn house, and if she ain't never met my daddy then I don't know why we're sittin' here wastin' each other's time." Sunny was silent, looking back and forth between Maisy and her mother as if she were watching a tennis match. She began wondering if this *had* been a mistake. Perhaps Maisy was insane after all.

Maisy knew the conversation would get contentious, but she never wavered. "It's true. Theora never met Howard, but she knew Violet. She knew your mother."

"Hold on. At the cemetery you said you held me as a baby," Willow said, directing her statement at Theora who was still rocking in her chair. "Yeah, you said you held me and you held Sunny."

"You did what, now?" Hearing her name jolted Sunny back into the conversation.

Maisy nodded. "Yes, that is true. Violet brought you here when you were first born. She lied to Howard and said she was taking you to a doctor's checkup, but really she came here. Theora made a necklace from heather and put it around your neck. And when Sunny was born, she did the same with her."

"What kind of voodoo bullshit are you—"

"Heather," Sunny said, visibly racking her brain for the answer. "Heather means protection. It was a way to keep us safe!" She was proud to use her new knowledge on flower meanings.

Theora smiled, pointing to Sunny while addressing Willow. "The Sunflower is a smart one, yes?"

Maisy continued, "That's right, Sunny. The strand of braided heather was our way of wishing you safety from all the dangers in your lives. There was little else we could do at that time. Willow, I know you don't want to believe anything bad about your father, but I promised your mother I would help you see. Theora can help you see."

Willow sat back in her chair. "I have no idea what's going on right now. None of this is helping me." She looked at Sunny. "Seriously, why are we here?"

Sunny shrugged, worried the situation was getting out of control. "I don't—"

"When I was a girl," Theora began, cutting Sunny off, "I traveled the world with my father. We saw many marvelous places and met many peculiar people, but my favorite people were the Orientals. Now I know you aren't supposed to say that anymore, but that's what we called them back then. In 1920, when I was just a child of sixteen, my father and I set off for Vietnam. He was a businessman but very secretive about his work. In all my life I never actually knew what his job was, but I didn't mind as long as he let me come along on his journeys.

"I thought it must be the most exciting place in the world when we first arrived in Saigon. It was unlike any place I had ever seen before. It was nothing like London or Paris. I was instantly in love with everything about it. We were to stay there in Saigon for three weeks before departing for our next stop, I believe somewhere in Japan, but my father grew ill. The expensive doctors at the hospital could not figure out how to fix him, and I feared he might die. I asked a local shopkeeper, with whom I had grown friendly, what I should do and he suggested taking my father to a small Hoa village outside of the city. There was a man there, a medicine man, that he was sure could help my father. It was a race against time, as my father's condition began getting much worse." Theora stopped and pointed to the table with her cane, prompting Maisy to get her a cup of tea. "The shopkeep and his brother helped me get my father to the village because by then he could barely walk on his own. That is where I met him.

"'I am Chen Feng,' he said. 'I am doctor.' It was the only English he knew. Did you know I called him Chen for several days before I learned that they say last name before first name?"

"Theora, I had no idea," Willow replied. Her response was quite sarcastic but purely as a reflex. She hoped it hadn't come across as rude, because she was truly captivated by the story.

"It's true!" Theora said with a slight chuckle. "His name was Feng Chen, but they say it backwards. He was an immigrant from southeast China, as were most of the people in the village. They had all left their homeland because they did not agree with Chinese rule. Feng was a village elder and a truly wise man. He spoke Cantonese most of the time but he also knew French. It just so happened that I brought with me a French dictionary that my father had given me for my birthday that year. Using that I was able to explain to him why we had come. He spent a whole day with my father just talking, with me trying to translate, so that Feng could understand his ailments. Then he mixed up a tea for him to drink and an ointment for him to apply to his arms and legs, and within two days my father was cured. It was a miracle or maybe magic. I just knew that I needed to know how. How could a man be so sick one day and the next he is fine? All Feng used were plants! His home looked more like a garden shop than a doctor's office. Of course, he wasn't a *real* doctor, no. He never went to a medical school or any school that I know of. But he knew how to heal the human body because his family had been healers for generations, and all I wanted was to be able to do the same.

"When my father said it was time for us to leave, I begged him to let me stay. I couldn't imagine leaving before I knew how Feng had cured him. My father and I argued terribly. His business would not let him stay in Vietnam any longer, and I simply refused to go with him.

So I stayed. I stayed in the village with Feng, and I became his apprentice."

"Wait. Sorry. Time-out," Sunny said while forming her hands in a T-shape. "Your father just *left* you in a foreign country when you were sixteen?!" She couldn't believe it. It sounded so wild and went against everything she had ever pictured about the life of a teenager in the 1920s.

"He did! Isn't that something? Oh, but I loved it so much there. Living with Feng helped me learn French much quicker than reading that silly old dictionary. And I even taught him some English! And the villagers. Oh the villagers took me in as one of their own. Their way of life, it spoke to me unlike any other place I had visited. I felt more at home there than I did in Chicago, which is where I had been raised. I stayed with Feng until he died in 1932. It was hard to live there without him, because I had nobody to make me laugh anymore. He may have been a wise man, but he was quite clumsy. On many occasions he would knock things over or trip over his own feet. He had a good sense of humor about it all, which made me laugh even harder with him. One day he actually set his house on fire! Luckily we were able to pour the water on it before it burnt us all up. And do you know what he would do when the village children would come to him whining about an injury?"

Willow and Sunny both shook their heads as Willow asked, "What'd he do?" They were both leaning slightly forward in their seats, hanging on her every word. There was something hypnotic about Theora's slow calming voice.

"He would ask them, 'where does it hurt?', and when they would point to their arm or their knee he would flick them on that spot! Oh how the children would shriek as if he had caused them such pain! Feng would laugh and laugh as the children ran back to their homes." Theora took a sip of her tea and grinned thinking about the antics of Feng Chen.

"Dang! Feng was cold-blooded!" Willow said laughing.

"I eventually came back to the States in 1943. Saigon was getting too dangerous, and everyone began leaving the village. I came to Tennessee to be closer to my sister. I tried living in town, but it was simply too busy for me."

"You mean our town that only has one stoplight?" Sunny asked.

"Yes, that's the one. I've lived in these mountains ever since, helping this small village with medical care. Nobody up here can afford the big hospitals or doctors anymore. I don't charge them any money, and in exchange my village sees to it that I am cared for as well." Theora patted her lap with her hands as a sign she was finished with her story. She picked up her tea and began sipping, waiting for someone else to continue the conversation.

"That is a damn fine story, Miss Theora. For real. I surely did enjoy that. But again I have to ask, how the hell does any of this help me?" Willow was no longer impatient and short tempered, but rather genuinely curious as to why Maisy had brought them to Theora.

Maisy spoke up, "You have only witnessed your mother and father through *your* eyes. And a child's eyes are inherently biased in many ways. Theora has a way of changing your views so that you can experience memories through another's eyes."

Theora smiled. "Feng called it 'reliving tea' because you get to relive moments of your life and see them in a new way. It was one of the last things he taught me, but I rarely allow others to experience it. It can be far too dangerous for the emotions. Tell me Willow, do you like to live dangerously?" she asked, with a hint of mischief in her voice.

"I'm startin' to like you more and more, Theora. I think we could be good friends, you know, if I didn't have to look at you too often. No offense." Willow was obviously warming up to her.

"None taken. There's a reason I don't have a mirror in my home."

Maisy shushed her. "Theora, you have to take this seriously!"

This caused Theora and Willow to both laugh. "Oh, sweet Maisy. Always wanting me to be a mysterious witch casting spells on people. It is healthy to be silly. Feng Chen taught me that. I am not ashamed of my age or my appearance. I don't plan to win any beauty contest, but I'm proud to be me and all that I am. Too much serious is hurtful to your soul. Wrinkles are a sign of wisdom. Smooth skin is a sign of ignorance." She looked at Sunny and Willow and added, "No offense."

Sunny looked at Maisy and began speaking, ignoring the back-and-forth between Willow and Theora. "Okay, so you're going to make us some tea and we'll be able to—"

"Only Willow," Maisy interrupted. "You were not there, Sunflower."

"Please, for the love of God, just call me Sunny."

Maisy nodded. "Of course. I apologize, Sunny. You will not have the tea because your mind is already opened to learning about who Howard and Violet really were. Willow has yet to release herself from the memories that continue to haunt her. The tea is the only way for her to see what she was too young to notice."

"You keep saying she's going to *see* things. What do you mean by that?" Sunny asked.

"After drinking the tea she will begin to meditate, and once she is in a deep sleep she will see certain memories as if she were watching a movie of her life. Much like a dream that is so clear you would swear it was real." Maisy looked to Theora. "The recipe calls for specific ingredients to make this happen, but only Theora knows what they are."

Theora nodded. "If you agree to drink the tea to relive your memories, I will begin brewing some now."

Sunny and Willow looked at each other. Sunny was obviously unsure, but Willow was feeling adventurous. "Alright, Theora. Let's have some tea."

With a slight smile on her face, Theora looked to Maisy and said, "Bring three mushrooms up from the root cellar."

"Mushrooms?" Willow's eyes lit up. "Wait, are we doin' shrooms, Theora?! Awww, shit! I ain't tripped in years! You didn't need to tell me a story about your whole life with the China man. You coulda stole my heart with some shrooms the moment I walked in here!"

Maisy had left the room, but Theora looked at Willow with a puzzled expression and said, "This will not be the fun trip you are used to. Though I do have plenty of those mushrooms." Theora leaned closer to Willow and winked, whispering, *"We can talk about those later."*

Sunny rolled her eyes, embarrassed by her mother's behavior. "I think maybe just the tea is fine for now. Get a hold of yourself, mom. Christ almighty, you practically jumped out of your seat at the idea of getting high."

"Mushrooms are a totally different experience, Sun! It's not like gettin' messed up on pills. It's a journey unlike any other. Right, Theora?" Theora nodded. "See? She knows what I'm talkin' about! Up high, Theo!" Willow raised her hand expecting a high-five from her new, yet extremely old friend. Instead Theora simply smiled, reached out, and lightly gripped Willow's hand causing Sunny to laugh at the absolute ridiculousness of the situation they found themselves in.

Maisy returned with three mushrooms and placed them on the table. Despite being over one hundred years old, Theora stood up and walked across the room to an apothecary shelf that was completely covered in jars containing various plants, spices, and rocks. Each jar was labeled, and the entire shelf was meticulously organized. Theora made her way back to the table with several jars, including a few that were labeled in Hanzi, the traditional Chinese script she had learned from Feng Chen. After pouring water into her cast iron pot over the fire, she began cutting up the mushrooms and adding them into the pot. Next, she took bits and pieces from the Hanzi labeled jars. Sunny had been keenly watching everything Theora was doing and quickly asked about the contents of those jars.

"There is a reason I keep them in the old script. I told you, this tea could bring bad things if put in the wrong hands. Feng's recipe is secret, and I will take it with me to the grave." Theora was no longer as light-hearted as she was moments before. When she was performing her duties as a "doctor" she was stern. As she added more leaves and spices, there was no doubt she knew her way around a mortar and pestle. With everything crushed and mixed together, she poured it all in with the now boiling water and mushrooms.

"So how long does this need to cook before I can drink it?" Willow asked. She was suddenly feeling a bit unsure, but the urge to trip was all the motivation she needed to proceed.

Maisy spoke up while Theora stirred the pot. "First, you must decide on the memories you would like to visit. It is best to focus on times you can see clearly in your mind. They can be happy memories or sad. Memories that make you feel good or angry. Can you think of specific moments like that?"

Willow scoffed. "I can think of a million things that make me angry. Like this one time, when I was—"

"*Aw, hell-dern-shit!*" Theora cursed loudly, startling everyone in the room. "Bring me the jar of sassafras root from the shelf. Hurry, hurry!"

Sunny did as she was told. She grabbed the sassafras root and brought it to Theora. "Is this an important ingredient? Is it all ruined? I mean, is it still going to work?"

"Huh? Oh, yes. It's fine. But it tastes better with a hint of sassafras."

Maisy shook her head and rolled her eyes, exhausted by Theora's shenanigans. "You were saying, Willow?"

"Well, this one time when I's maybe six or seven, I got mama to sign me up for dance lessons up town. I was so excited. I just knew I was born to be a ballerina. Then the day of my first lesson, we didn't go. She said it was too much money and it was best if we waited another year or two. I mean, there I was sittin' by the door ready to go. It must have been a pitiful sight to see." Willow had started wringing her hands as she told the story. Sunny was worried it was all getting to be too much for her.

"This is good, Willow. Think of a few more of those vivid memories. I know it can be difficult, but it will help your trip that much more. You must focus on those memories. Every detail from every one of your senses. What were you seeing? Where were you and what was around you? What did you hear? What could you smell? What were you feeling, both physically and emotionally? Everything is important for this experience to help you understand. The more details you remember, the more you will see from that time period." Maisy's intensity was interlaced with her sincerity. It was obvious she cared deeply about Willow and wanted her journey to be successful.

Sunny was still having second thoughts. "Mom, are you feeling okay about all this? I mean, you don't have to do it if you don't want to. I'm sure we can just talk about mamaw and grampa and the house. Nobody will be upset if you—"

"Stop treatin' me like a child, Sunny. I trust my girl, Theora." Willow's attitude was becoming not unlike her most reckless times, causing Sunny to worry even more. She could tell Willow was scared and focusing only on the opportunity to get high. The all-but-guaranteed emotional toll of this process had been lost on her.

Maisy tried to steer her back on track. "Make sure you are thinking of memories from many times in your life at the farm and not just one age or one event. This trip can only be taken once, so you must discover it all now."

"Why only once? What happens if you do it again?" Sunny asked.

"You go crazy," Theora replied matter-of-factly. "At least that's what Feng warned of. I didn't dare test it in order to find out. He said reliving more than once will cause the mind to get lost between the then and the now, forever confusing your sense of dream and reality."

Willow perked up. "Dang, Theora. What kind of mushrooms are those?"

"The mushrooms remain a mystery even to me. I grow them in my root cellar, as they do not grow here naturally. I brought them with me from our village in Vietnam. Feng had brought them from his home in China. It was the one ingredient he did not give me a name for, so I couldn't provide the full recipe even if I tried."

"Hold on. Are we sure this is safe? I mean, my mom has done a lot of drugs in her life. Like, *a lot* of drugs. What if she somehow already ate this type of mushroom before and that causes her to lose her mind? This is all starting to sound somewhat iffy to me." Suddenly, Sunny wished she had never found the hidden key. This was all happening because of her inability to walk away from an unsolved mystery. She thought about how she could be in Scotland right now with Finn and Lil, touring a castle or seeing some Highland cows grazing in a field, but it was too late now. Instead she was stuck in a mountain shack in Tennessee with a witch doctor brewing up some sort of psilocybin tea while her husband, with whom she was now fighting, and daughter were thousands of miles away buying livestock.

Theora grinned her mischievous grin while ladling the mixture into an archaic tea press and said, "Only one way to find out, yes Willow?"

Willow and Sunny looked at each other. The inflection in Theora's voice had given them both chills, and they watched as she filled a delicate teacup adorned with an exquisite floral pattern. The steam rising out of the cup created mesmerizing swirls engaging in a silent bolero toward the ceiling. Willow scooted her chair closer to the table, never taking her eyes off of the cup.

"Okay, so I just drink this and then I'll start trippin'?"

Maisy shook her head. "It will take a bit of time to really kick in, but once you have finished the entire cup you must lay down and begin your meditation. You must focus on those memories and *only* those memories. Do you understand?"

"Yeah, I get it. How long will the trip last?" Willow asked, still not looking away from the teacup.

"Is there somewhere else you need to be?" Theora asked. "Every trip is different. Some trips last minutes. Some last hours. Feng told me of a trip that lasted days. This is not an exact science."

"*Days?!* How much tea did that person drink?" Sunny asked.

"Perhaps too much," Theora said. She then stood up from the table and went back to her rocking chair. Once comfortable, she closed her eyes and rested.

"Mom, are you really sure you want to—" Before Sunny could finish her question Willow began drinking the tea.

Sunny watched her intently. After a few sips, Willow said, "It actually tastes great. A little like root beer."

"Sassafras!" Theora exclaimed, eyes still closed.

"Go to sleep, Theora!" Maisy scolded. "We must be completely silent once the tea is finished so that Willow can concentrate."

Theora opened her eyes and looked at Maisy. "You act like I don't know how this works. I ought to whack you with this cane."

Willow looked at the cane, while still sipping the tea. "I actually wanted to ask you about that thing ever since that terrifying day in the cemetery. Where did you get it? All the dragons and shit carved into it. It's really badass."

"It belonged to Feng Chen, and it was made by his grandfather." Theora smiled while admiring the intricate details.

Willow's eyes grew wide. "Oh man, so that's like a crazy old antique."

Maisy was getting increasingly aggravated by the conversation. "You must stop this at once. Willow, focus on your memories. Theora, go to sleep. Sunny, would you like a glass of water?"

Sunny sat up straighter when hearing her name, assuming she was getting reprimanded as well. "What? Oh no, thank you. I'm fine."

Willow carefully sat the empty teacup down on its matching saucer. "Okay, I'm done. What next?"

Maisy stood up and pointed to the cot next to the wall. "You must rest. Close your eyes, and meditate on the memories you have chosen. Think of nothing else. Do not let other visions enter your mind."

Willow went to the cot and sat down. "What if I don't know how to meditate?"

"You're a hippie aren't you?" Maisy asked.

"Oh yeah. Far out." With that, Willow laid her head on the pillow and closed her eyes.

Sunny looked back at Maisy and awkwardly smiled, knowing they could only sit and wait in silence as Theora lightly snored next to the fireplace.

*A dark room. . . . . BUMP-BUMP. . . . . chaotic piano tones. . . . .
distant voices. . . . . Oh my darlin. . . . . a voice whispers, "Quiet,
little mouse". . . . . soft blankets. . . . . angry voices. . . . . BUMP-
BUMP. . . . . inhale. . . . . crickets chirping. . . . . smeared red
lipstick. . . . . pink tulle on a hardwood floor. . . . . cozy and warm. . . .
. BUMP-BUMP. . . . . fresh nighttime air. . . . . Oh my darlin. . . . .
exhale. . . . . shouts of rage. . . . . a white shirt blowing in the breeze. .
. . . . broken glass. . . . . BUMP-BUMP. . . . . silence. . . . . Oh my
darlin, Clementine. . . . . a polka dot mouse. . . . . sun tea brewing in
the garden. . . . . inhale. . . . . an empty table. . . . . exhale. . . . .*

A heartbeat echoes like soldiers' footsteps marching in time. . . . .
BUMP-BUMP. . . . . Willow sleeps soundly beneath the soft blankets
covering her bed. Her dreams are peaceful. . . . . *You are lost and
gone forever* . . . . Beyond the slumbering bedroom are the voices of
Violet and Howard. What they say is unclear, but the emotions are
unmistakable. Howard screams at her as a bottle breaks. The door
slams and his truck engine roars to life. The sound of the tires against
the gravel driveway fills the night air. Violet begins sweeping up the
broken glass that has shattered on the kitchen floor. The march of the

heartbeat does not care. It obscures the noises so that Willow's sleep is undisturbed. . . . . *silence.*

Sunlight pierces through a window. . . . . BUMP-BUMP. . . . . teardrops on a pillow. . . . . tall flowers, pink and purple. . . . . inhale. . . . . bright, marble eyes. . . . . "Shhh! The cat is near!". . . . . BUMP-BUMP. . . . .red velvet stained with tears. . . . . a feeling of deceit. . . . . BUMP-BUMP, BUMP-BUMP. . . . . blinking babydoll. . . . . exhale. . . . . empty chairs around a table. . . . . creaking wood under footsteps. . . . . Oh my darlin. . . . . BUMP-BUMP. . . . . pink tulle piled on the floor. . . . . a door slams. . . . .

Willow sits quietly in her homemade pink tutu by the door, so excited she can barely sit still. She wonders if the other girls will like her. She wonders if she'll fit in. She imagines herself on a stage performing leaps and pirouettes while an orchestra plays and the crowd admires her talent. In her mind she is a real ballerina. Violet enters the room, and her face is full of sadness. . . . . *Inhale.*

"I'm so sorry, sweet girl. We cannot take dance lessons this year. We simply don't have enough money right now. I am so very sorry, dear. I know you were really looking forward to this."

Willow's eyes fill with tears as anger and confusion flood her tiny body. "But you promised, mama! You promised!"

Violet holds back her own tears. She feels a pain far worse than that of Willow's. . . . . *Oh my darlin.* . . . . "I can teach you everything I know about dance. I used to be pretty good when I was a young girl." Her smile is forced. She knows she has broken her daughter's heart. . . . . *Exhale.*

Willow pushes past her and runs up the stairs to her room, slamming the door. She rips off the pink tutu and throws it to the floor before burying her face in her pillow. Violet is left alone in the sitting room. She stumbles back onto the red velvet couch, unable to withstand the weight of her sorrow.

Howard enters the room and scoffs. "Cryin' over dance lessons. Last thing I need is a daughter runnin' around town dancin' like some harlot. She ought to be learnin' her manners and becomin' a respectable young lady."

"She's just a child!" Violet cries.

"Yeah, she's my child!" Howard snaps. . . . . *BUMP-BUMP, BUMP-BUMP.* . . . . Before Violet can reply he continues, "And you used *my* money to sign up for these damned classes. You can twirl your ass right back into town and get every penny back from that teacher.". . . . . *Oh my darlin, Clementine.*

Bubbles floating in the sunlight. . . . . splish-splash-splosh. . . . . an empty table. . . . . BUMP-BUMP. . . . . red lipstick. . . . . a tractor engine grumbles, POP-POP-POP-POP. . . . . swinging in the breeze. . . . . a washtub full of clothes. . . . . sun tea brewing in the garden. . . . . Oh my darlin, Clementine. . . . . soft blankets. . . . . blinking babydoll. . . . . a clap, a thud. . . . . candles burning bright. . . . . BUMP-BUMP. . . . . clothespins in a basket. . . . . a single voice sings. . . . . a clean, white shirt hangs in the sunlight. . . . .

Willow lays on the porch swing. The breeze feels good on her skin. Howard is on the tractor in the field working with the old farmer from next door and his son, Archie. Not allowed to help with the farming chores, Willow rests on the swing instead, watching Violet scrub the laundry from the previous week. . . . . *splish-splash-splosh.* . . . . The giant basin, full of sudsy water, is in direct sunlight. Violet wipes her brow of sweat and arches her back. Scrubbing the garments, wringing them with her hands, and hanging them on the clothesline is a strenuous job and one that taxes her body like no other. Willow's eyes grow heavy. Before succumbing to her afternoon nap, she notices her father's white button-up shirt is next on the pile to be washed. . . . . *BUMP-BUMP.* . . . . A smear of red lipstick on the collar is impossible to miss. She watches her mother scrub it clean, wondering why she would be so careless as to get lipstick on his shirt knowing she would have to be the one to wash it later. But the stained collar does not phase Violet, despite never wearing lipstick herself. . . . . *BUMP-BUMP.* . . . . His unfaithfulness does not surprise her, for she has known all along. Violet hangs the shirt on the line and picks up the next piece to be washed. She sees Willow sleeping on the swing and smiles.

A child giggles. . . . . BUMP-BUMP. . . . . gentle resistance of the smooth white and black keys. . . . . inhale. . . . . a clap, a thud. . . . .long, blinking eyelashes. . . . . an angry voice in the distance. . . . . sunlight on a frustrated face. . . . . "Shhh! The cat is near!". . . . . small feet dangling beneath a wooden bench. . . . . BUMP-BUMP. . . . . a polka dot mouse. . . . . smoke rising toward the ceiling. . . . . exhale. . . . . a painful cry. . . . . You are lost and gone forever. . . . . glass shatters. . . . . a familiar tune. . . . .

The sound of the piano is soothing. The song is familiar but unnamed. Willow tiptoes into the room to find Violet at the bench, her hands floating effortlessly across the keys. She sits down next to her and watches as her mother finishes the song.

Willow says, "I want to play."

Violet smiles. . . . . *Oh my darlin, Clementine.* . . . . She is eager to teach her daughter on her grandmother's piano. "It takes a lot of practice, my dear. We can start our first lesson if you would like."

Before she can say another word Willow hits the keys randomly, sending a lively and chaotic song throughout the house. They both giggle. From another room, Howard's thundering voice curses the noise. . . . . *"In the mouse's house. Hurry, hurry!".* . . . . and Violet grows tense. She pulls Willow close and removes her hands from the piano. "We mustn't play now, Willow. We will try another day, yes?"

Willow is angry and forcefully pulls away from her, running out of the room and onto the front porch. She holds in a frustrated scream as the sunlight washes over her. Violet hangs her head, and closes the fallboard as Howard yells out, "The next time I hear that goddamned piano, I'm taking an ax to it!". . . . . *"Quiet, little mouse."*

A light sheet brushes against bare skin. . . . . BUMP-BUMP. . . . . crickets chirping. . . . . thick, humid air. . . . . blinking babydoll. . . . . angry voices. . . . . wood creaking under footsteps. . . . . pink tulle on a hardwood floor. . . . . Oh my darlin. . . . . BUMP-BUMP. . . . . smeared red lipstick. . . . . chaotic piano tones. . . . . sun tea brewing in the garden. . . . . inhale. . . . . a silent piano. . . . . teardrops on a pillow. . . . . exhale. . . . .

The bedroom is dark except for the small lamp on the bedside table. Willow is reading a book well past her bedtime. Downstairs the voices have grown louder. Howard and Violet are speaking in biting tones.

"But why can't I?" asks Violet.

"You have no business leaving the house all day. Getting a job? You've lost your goddamned mind. The minute I let you get a job is the day you try and leave me." Howard is sitting in his chair, beads of sweat cascade down from his temples. It is summertime and the air outside is calm. Without a breeze to pass through the windows, the house feels like a sauna.

"If leaving was my plan I would have gone long ago, Howard. But you made sure that that never happened, didn't you? You've kept me in this prison for years! Now I can't even—"

"Prison?!" Howard's eyes fill with fury as he turns to look at her. . . . . *Oh my darlin, Clementine.* . . . . "You think this is a prison, do you?" He stands up and walks across the room to where Violet sits on the couch. She shrinks away from him. He leans down close to her face, his arms on either side of her body. She is trapped. His voice is calm, but menacing. "I can make this a real prison if need be. You know that, don't you? I'm the one keepin' food on the table. I'm the one keepin' this farm operatin'. Hell, soon I'll be the one keepin' the whole damn town runnin'. And I can't do that if people think I can't manage my own family. You ought to be grateful for the life I've given you. Without me you'd be a disgrace. A disgusting, filthy, whore." He spits on her and returns to his chair. . . . . *You are lost and gone forever.* . . . . Violet remains silent. She pulls a handkerchief embroidered with small green and yellow oak leaves from her apron pocket and uses it to wipe her face clean, as Willow drifts off to sleep. . . . . *Dreadful sorrow, Clementine.*

An empty table. . . . . BUMP-BUMP. . . . . *chaotic piano tones.* . . . . *Oh my darlin, Clementine.* . . . . *angry voices.* . . . . *a clap, a thud.* . . . . *candles burning bright.* . . . . BUMP-BUMP. . . . . *blinking babydoll.* . . . . *the smell of freshly baked cake.* . . . . *bright marble eyes.* . . . . *sun tea in the garden.* . . . . *You are lost and gone forever.* . . . . *smeared red lipstick.* . . . . *a lonely wish.* . . . . .

The dining room is empty. Willow sits at the head of the table. The lamps are turned off and the only light is from the sun bleeding in from the next room's windows. She hears her mother moving around in the kitchen before she joins her in the dining room.

"Happy birthday to you! Happy birthday to you!" Violet's lone voice bounces off the walls while Willow watches her carry in a small cake with ten candles shining bright. "Happy birthday, my dear Willow! Happy birthday to you!" Violet places the cake on the empty table in front of her daughter. . . . . *Inhale.* . . . . "Blow out the candles and make a wish, darling!"

While Violet stands next to her, beaming with pride at the beautiful young girl her daughter has become, Willow does as she's told and closes her eyes tight. . . . . *Exhale.* . . . . She wishes for a party filled with friends and family. She opens her eyes to find that the room is still empty except for her mother and the smoke rising toward the ceiling. She slumps back in the chair. They sit together at the table eating the small homemade cake. Just as they finish the last few bites, Violet perks up in her seat when she hears Howard's truck pulling in the driveway. She knows where he's been and she knows what state of mind he is in. . . . . *"Into the mouse's house! Hurry, hurry!"*

"Willow, can you run out and check on the sun tea in the garden? Go on out the front door. Hurry up now. We don't want it brewing too long out there." Violet looks back toward the kitchen where she knows Howard will enter. She turns back to make sure Willow is outside before their paths can cross.

Howard slams the door behind him. . . . . *"Quiet, little mouse". . . . .* He yells at Violet, "You spent eight dollars on a damn dress?! Eight dollars! Have you lost your ever-lovin' mind?!"

"It's a gift for Willow's birthday, Howard! She can't go through her whole life wearing the rags that I sew together for her. She's ten years old. She deserves to have a nice dress to wear—"

Howard crosses the room and shoves Violet against the wall, his hand around her throat. . . . . *Oh my darlin.* . . . . "She deserves a house to live in and food on the table. If she wants something more than that she can do extra chores and earn an allowance. Come to think of it, maybe you need to do some extra chores around here. Drop down on your knees every once in a while and maybe I'll give you a little spendin' money.". . . . . *Oh my darlin.* . . . . His menacing smile of crooked teeth does nothing to shield her from the whiskey on his breath. Violet sees Willow approaching the house with the sun tea and tries shoving him away, motioning toward the door. Realizing Willow is close by, he releases her and Violet leaves the room, coughing and trying to catch her breath. . . . . *Oh my darlin, Clementine.*

"Hey, daddy!" Willow says as she places the tea on the table.

"Well if it isn't my birthday girl! How old are you now, sixteen? Seventeen?"

"Daddy! I'm ten!" Willow giggles and rolls her eyes.

Howard reaches into his pocket and pulls out three dollars. "Happy birthday, Willow. Go hide this here money from your mama. Lord knows she'll try and take it to town to buy somethin' foolish."

Willow's eyes light up as she grabs the money from his hand. "Oh thank you, daddy! Thank you so much!" She turns and runs to her room.

Violet returns to the kitchen holding the dress she bought, still wrapped with a bow. She looks at Howard as he says, "Take it back to the store. Now.". . . . . *You are lost and gone forever.*

A full moon. . . . . a blinking babydoll. . . . . BUMP-BUMP. . . . .
tall flowers, pink and purple. . . . . Oh my darlin. . . . . angry
voices. . . . . "Into the mouse's house! Hurry, hurry!". . . . . BUMP-
BUMP. . . . . chaotic piano tones. . . . . a polka dot mouse. . . . . Oh my
darlin, Clementine. . . . . a clap, a thud. . . . . "Shhhh! The mouse is
near!". . . . . BUMP-BUMP. . . . .pink tulle on a hardwood floor. . . . .
You are lost and gone forever. . . . . crickets chirping. . . . . a soft
blanket. . . . . a rosy cheek. . . . .

The hour is late and the moon is full. The evening breeze blows freely through the farmhouse. Violet closes the window closest to her to keep from getting too cold. Three-year-old Willow sits on the floor next to her mother playing with a babydoll. It is made of hard plastic with long eyelashes and marble-like eyes. Willow giggles each time she tilts the babydoll backwards and sees its little eyelids close. Violet's face is beaming, joyful that her daughter is so delighted with the toy. The babydoll is one of the only store-bought toys that Willow has. All of her other toys are homemade stuffed animals sewn together from leftover pieces of fabric and stuffed with cotton balls. It isn't much, but Willow is a happy child.

Headlights shine through the window, casting a spotlight on the floral wallpaper and dancing around the room before exiting. Violet is on her feet. She peers out the window and sees Howard stumble out of his truck. He yells out her name in anger. Her demeanor changes in an instant as she scoops Willow up in her arms and rushes from the living room into the study.

"We're going to play a game now, baby girl." She is speaking with an urgency that is also soothing to Willow's young ears. Walking behind the desk to the corner of the room, she kneels down and opens a small panel revealing a hidden nook in the wall. Inside is a silver flashlight, a small blanket, and a stuffed animal mouse that is made from the scraps of Willow's polka dot dress. "Quiet as a mouse, sweet Willow," Violet says as she turns on the record player to Willow's favorite song. . . . . *Oh my darlin, Oh my darlin, Oh my darlin, Clementine.* . . . . She turns it up louder than normal, hearing Howard entering into the kitchen. "Into the mouse's house! Hurry, hurry!" Willow crawls into the secret nook with her babydoll and turns on the flashlight. The light lands across the room to several vases of heather, and she admires the bright pink and purple flowers rising up like flames on the shelf. She picks up the little mouse and hugs it tight against her chest saying, "Quiet, little mouse." Before closing the panel, Violet grabs a few sprigs of heather from a vase on the window sill and lays them next to Willow. She smiles at her daughter before shutting the panel in an effort to reassure her that this is simply a game. She quickly leaves the room, closing the door behind her.

Willow rocks her babydoll with the same care and tenderness of a new mother. She reaches out and pets the mouse, covering it with part of the blanket. "Quiet as a mouse," she whispers to her babydoll. She hums along with the record rocking back and forth, determined to get her babydoll to sleep. Her ears are focusing on her favorite song, but it is impossible to completely drown out the terror unfolding in the kitchen.

Howard is standing in the doorway. Violet is on the other side of the small table in the center of the room. She asks him how his day was, praying he's only drunk and not drunk and angry.

"My day? Oh my day was swell, darlin'. How was *your* day?" His words are slurred and he sways back and forth as he speaks. His tone is eerily playful and sarcastic.

She answers cautiously. "Just a normal day I suppose. I had a checkup at the doctor's office. Everything is fine, though. I saved you a plate from supper. Can I heat it up for you?"

His face grows rigid and his eyes narrow in on her face. "Doctor's appointment, huh? That's where you was all day?"

She smiles weakly. "That's right. Willow wasn't too fussy which made going out much easier. She even—"

"Where's the baby now?" he asks, cutting her off.

Her heart sinks. It is obvious she's scared. "She's in her room, sleeping."

"Tell me somethin', Vi. What doctor of yours is up in the mountains?" A sinister grin has taken over his face. He has her trapped. She doesn't answer. "Yeah, how 'bout that? Couple of the boys said they seen you drivin' out of the mountains this afternoon. Now last I checked Doc Emerson's office ain't up in the mountains." His grin is slowly morphing into a look of rageful disgust.

Violet begins stumbling over her words, her hands shake as she tries desperately to keep her whole body from trembling in fear. "It w-w-was such a pretty day out. I-I-I just thought Willow would like to drive into the mountains for a little while. That's all—"

"*BULLSHIT!*" he screams, shoving the table out of the way as he races toward her. Violet runs to the pantry hoping to escape through the back door, but he's quick to catch her.

In the study, behind the faux wall panel Willow lays her babydoll down and covers it up with a blanket. She curls up next to it and pets the little mouse. "Shhhh! The cat is near!" she whispers.

Howard pulls Violet back into the kitchen and shoves her against the wall. She is crying, desperate to get away from him. He easily overpowers her, gripping her arms as he holds her against the wall. "WHO WERE YOU MEETING IN THE MOUNTAINS?! HUH? TELL ME, GODDAMMIT!"

"Nobody!" she cries. "We simply went for a drive, Howard!" She stops resisting, realizing her efforts are futile.

"LIAR!" He strikes her across the face with the back of his hand. . . . . *You are lost and gone forever.* . . . . . Her knees weaken, but he holds her up. He smells strongly of whiskey, as if the sweat seeping from his body is straight from the bottle he drank earlier.

"No! Please, no more!" she begs. She holds her hands up to her cheek, now throbbing in pain.

He lets go of her and unbuckles his belt. She tries to get away again, but he trips her and she tumbles to the ground. The rage in his eyes has turned to madness. He pulls his belt off, staring at her as she attempts to crawl away from him. He raises his arm and brings it down with all his might. The leather lands across her back. . . . . *a clap.* . . . . and she falls flat against the floor. . . . . *a thud.* . . . . She cries out and curls into the fetal position as he continues to whip her until his arm tires.

As he puts his belt back on he says, "Lie to me again, Vi, and you'll see what happens when I really get angry." He steps over her and walks to the door. "Clean yourself up and get this house back in order before I get home tomorrow. I'm no longer in the mood to share a bed with a lyin' whore like you tonight." As he walks outside he says over his shoulder, "Luckily I have a wonderful friend in town that can satisfy all my needs.". . . . *smeared red lipstick.* . . . . His footsteps recede and the sound of his truck engine fades into the night.

Violet gathers all of her strength and rises to her feet. She goes to the powder room to look in the mirror. Her cheek is red and beginning to swell, but it won't be hard to cover with a little makeup. That is the only visible mark he has left on her except for what is hidden beneath her clothes. She carefully slips one arm out of her dress sleeve to reveal the fresh marks next to old scars across her ribcage. She is pleased to see that he hasn't drawn blood this time. Slowly, and using the wall to support her, she makes her way into the study. She winces in pain as she kneels down to open the hidden door. Willow smiles seeing her mother, and Violet smiles back at her. . . . . *Dreadful sorrow, Clementine.* . . . .

Sunny had fallen asleep with her head in her hand and her elbow resting on the table. Theora was silently rocking in her chair with her eyes unfocused, lost in a daydream. Maisy was knitting what appeared to be a scarf or perhaps the beginnings of a blanket. The shack had been silent for more than two hours. Willow was still on the cot. She had not moved since she began her meditation. The intensity of her fluctuating breath was the only indication that the reliving tea was doing its job.

Gasping for air as if she had been drowning, Willow suddenly sat up. It startled Sunny and Maisy, but Theora didn't so much as flinch and simply said with a smile, "You came back."

Sunny rushed to her mother's side. "Mom? Are you okay? Can you hear me?" She was rubbing Willow's back and holding onto her hand.

Willow nodded her head. "I'm okay." Her voice was soft, much like that of a child's. "I wanna go home." She looked at Theora and then to Maisy. She seemed to be scared of them and gripped Sunny tighter, her hands trembling.

Sunny looked at Maisy, afraid that something terrible had happened to her mother. "Is this normal? Is it okay for her to get up? I mean, what do we do now?"

Maisy stood up and walked around the table toward the bed. She didn't get too close because she knew Willow was frightened. "Take her home. She has experienced parts of her life that were buried many years ago. She will need time to recover. Do not ask her questions. Do not urge her to talk. Let her rest and reflect. You will know when the time is right to return."

"Return? You mean this isn't over?"

"No, dear Sunny. This is not over. The truth is only just beginning to unfold for you and Willow. Go now, and take care of your mother."

Sunny helped Willow to her feet and walked out of the shack, glancing behind her in the hopes Maisy or Theora would give her any sort of explanation for what had happened to her mother. They walked down the path toward Maisy's house. Willow's eyes were vacant, staring straight ahead, and her feet shuffled like a child cautiously walking across a frozen puddle. They drove back down the mountain without saying a word.

Upon entering the farmhouse, Willow walked straight to the living room and curled up on the couch. She slept throughout the day and into the night while Sunny sat on the recliner watching television and reading a book, never leaving her mother's side. When she finally woke up, Willow sat on the edge of the couch and looked around the room. Sunny watched her, unsure of what to say or do. Maisy had told her not to ask questions, but internally she was bursting with curiosity. There was so much she wanted to know. Instead, she told her mom she would go make her a sandwich for supper.

"No thank you, baby. I'm not hungry," Willow said. "I think I'm just gonna go to bed. I feel completely drained after all of this. I'm sure I'll feel better tomorrow."

"Are you sure?" She wondered if that counted as a type of question she wasn't supposed to ask. Willow ignored her and walked out of the room toward the stairs. "Umm, okay then. Goodnight, mom." Sunny decided she too would head off to bed. She had no idea what the next day would bring, but she wanted to be rested. She considered sleeping in the room with her mother but decided that might be too overprotective, not to mention harder for them both to rest comfortably while sharing a bed.

It was three o'clock in the morning when Willow got up. She walked down the hallway to the bathroom and splashed cold water on her face. As she passed by Sunny's bedroom she glanced in to find her sleeping soundly. She continued down the steps and through the sitting room, dragging her fingertips along the red velvet couch and envisioning her mother falling back on it in tears. Next she was in the dining room, staring at an empty table again and remembering the taste of the homemade cake. She made her way through the kitchen and into the study. The room was dark, so she turned on the desktop lamp. She hadn't noticed when she was in there before, but vases were scattered around the room. On the shelves, on the window sill, on the fireplace mantle. She remembered now that they had once been filled with heather. In her mind she could hear Sunny's voice echoing, *"Heather means protection."* Willow walked around the desk and knelt down in the corner. She slowly and cautiously placed her hands on the wall and opened the faux panel revealing the hidden nook.

Sunny woke up and rubbed her eyes. The morning sunlight crept in through the striped curtains as she sat up in bed and stretched. Before calling Finn and Lilias, she knew she needed to check on her mom and maybe get a pot of coffee started. Despite not drinking the previous night, Sunny felt somewhat hungover. She put her hair up in a ponytail, went to the bathroom, and then checked in Willow's room. She wasn't too surprised to find it empty seeing as how much Willow had slept the day before. Sunny called out to her mom as she walked down the stairs but she didn't receive an answer. Passing by the red velvet couch, she suddenly realized the house was silent and eerily still. Her heart began pounding. She looked in the living room, the dining room, the powder room. No signs of Willow. No breakfast had been prepared in the kitchen, no coffee had been brewed. The door to the study that usually stood open was now closed. Sunny walked toward it with a lump in her throat. She slowly turned the doorknob and opened the door. She let out a sigh of relief seeing that the study was also empty and undisturbed. But the relief was short-lived. Willow was obviously not in the house. Sunny looked out into the driveway to find that the rental car, her mother's car, and her grandfather's truck were all still parked in their usual spots. She called her mom's cell phone only to hear it ringing from the kitchen counter.

Sunny's mind was in a frenzy. She couldn't call the police. What could she possibly tell them about the situation she was in? Her mother had eaten a bunch of questionable mushrooms the day before that a witch in the mountains had smuggled into the country back in the 1920s that she got from an old Chinese man in Vietnam and now her mom had gone missing at some point over the last few hours? Of course, the local police would recognize Willow's name and probably wouldn't be all that surprised by the story, at least not the part about the mushrooms and the fact that she'd gone missing. For all Sunny knew there were still outstanding warrants for her mother's arrest over some long-forgotten charges from her younger and wilder years. She wondered who she could call or where she would even start looking. She hadn't been in this part of the world for many years, so she no longer knew where her mom might run off to. She no longer knew her mother's friends or coworkers. She no longer knew her dealers for that matter. Completely alone and on the verge of a full-blown panic attack, Sunny called the only person she could think of.

"Hey, Sun," Finn answered.

When she tried to speak, no words seemed to form. Sunny began crying into the phone. Her breath was rapid and she was nearly hyperventilating.

"Whoa, love. What's going on?! Calm down. It's going to be okay, love. Whatever it is. Sun, talk to me. Please." Finn was beginning to panic as well.

"She's gone. I can't— She just— I don't know where—"

Finn's fear subsided. He wasn't surprised that Willow would pull something like this again. His voice unintentionally took on a much more condescending tone. "I need you to breathe, Sunny. Inhale and exhale. Just like we tell Lil when she's throwing a tantrum. Practice your mindfulness, love."

"Oh, don't patronize me, Finley. Don't you dare! You have no idea what I'm dealing with right now. My God, you are unbelievable, you know that?!"

"I'm sorry, truly. But you have to see this from my point of view. This has *literally* happened before. This is just what she does. She disappears and goes on a bender for days at a time. At least this time we didn't entrust her with our bairn."

Sunny wiped her eyes. She refused to admit that he was right, because something felt different about this time. "I don't know how to find her, Finn. Everything has gotten out of hand here the last few days. There was a witch doctor and this mushroom tea and she started tripping, and—"

"The witch started tripping?" Finn asked.

"What? No! My mom was tripping. The witch just gave her the mushrooms."

"Aye, I see. Right. That makes much more sense. And how many did you eat, love?"

"Goddammit, Finn! This is serious! She was emotionally tortured yesterday and today she's missing!"

"I honestly dinnae ken how you expect *me* to help with this situation. You sound like a skyrocket, Sun."

"You know what? Fine. I'm sorry I bothered you. Just go back to your castle. I assume your mom has arranged an afternoon tea with the Queen and you mustn't be late!" She cursed him under her breath as she hung up and tossed her phone on the table. Looking around the room and wondering what to do next she realized she needed to eat and get some amount of caffeine in her system if she was going to be at all productive.

As Sunny prepared her breakfast she began thinking of the last time her mother went missing. She hadn't thought about that weekend in years, but Finn mentioning it had brought it to the forefront of her mind. Lilias was only seven months old when they came to introduce her to Willow. The plan had been for Sunny, Finley, and Lilias to spend the night in Knoxville with Willow and then Sunny and Finn would take off for a romantic one night getaway in a cabin in the mountains while Willow watched Lil. It was their first time being away from their daughter, but they were both exhausted and ready for a break. Willow was delighted to meet her granddaughter and the two of them bonded immediately. Watching the two of them sitting in the floor playing, Sunny had never seen her mother so full of joy.

Sunny and Finn arrived back at Willow's home just after lunchtime the following day only to find Lilias screaming in a playpen. The television was blaring out an infomercial while an unknown woman slept on the couch. Lilias was in desperate need of a diaper change and they had no idea when she last ate. There was no sign of Willow in the house. Sunny grabbed Lil, making sure she wasn't injured, and began changing her soiled clothing. Finley proceeded to scream at the lady passed out on the couch. Once the woman came to, she simply said that she and some friends had stopped by the previous night to talk to Willow and that was the last thing she remembered. Finn quickly kicked the woman out of the house, threatening to call the police.

After calming her down, Sunny started nursing Lilias. She was so angry she was shaking, but she was also scared that something terrible might have happened to her mother. Finley, on the other hand, was not at all worried about Willow's safety. He had never trusted her, and after seeing his young daughter screaming in the playpen he knew he never would.

"She should be locked up for this shite, Sun. One night! We asked her to be an adult for *one feckin' night*! Honestly, we have to get out of here afore she gets back because I could kill her right now. I'm that feckin' mad."

"I'm mad too, Finn! But Jesus, what if she was taken? I just can't believe she'd voluntarily leave her granddaughter here alone."

"Oh she dinnae leave her alone, love! She had a jakey passed out on the couch to keep her company!" As usual, his anger turned to over-the-top sarcasm mixed with Scottish slang. Sunny rarely knew what he was talking about.

"What do you want me to do, Finn? I'm taking care of our child which is the number one priority right now. Once she's fed and my boobs aren't about to burst, I can think clearly and we can figure out what to do next."

Inevitably, Finn won the argument and as soon as Lilias finished nursing, they packed their things up and headed back to New York. Sunny left a note on the counter asking Willow to call her the moment she returned home. For two days she waited by the phone in their apartment before she finally heard from her.

"Hello?" Sunny answered.

"Hi, Sunny girl. It's me and I'm so sor—"

"*Where the fuck have you been?!*" she screamed into the phone.

Willow began sobbing. "I'm so sorry, baby! There's no excuse good enough. I failed you and Finn and that sweet baby. I just—"

"*You're sorry?!* No. 'Sorry' is when you accidentally put a dent in the car. 'Sorry' is when you spill something on the carpet. 'Sorry' is *not* when you abandon a baby and disappear for *days*! *Days*, mom! *How could you?!*"

Willow tried to respond, but she knew there were no words that could fix this.

"Ya know, I hope it was worth it, mom. I hope whatever shithole you ended up in was full of the best drugs and you had the high of your life. Because that might be the last time you ever see your granddaughter. I'm so fucking angry right now, mom, but it doesn't even begin to compare to how angry Finley is. He still wants to call the police and report you for negligence. Just don't bother calling here again. I know you're alive and that's the only reason I wanted you to call. If I ever calm down from this, *maybe* I'll call you."

"No, baby. No please. I want to explain, please. *Please*, baby!" Willow had collapsed to the floor, desperate to not lose her daughter. The truth was that the people who had been to her house that night weren't exactly friends. It was her ex-boyfriend Jerry and a few of his buddies. Willow had a storage locker a few blocks away where Jerry had, without Willow's permission or knowledge, kept a large stash of marijuana. They promised to drive her there and back quickly so that she could return to her granddaughter. She refused at first, but she also knew Jerry was bad news and wanted him away from Lilias as soon as possible. She finally agreed as long as Jerry's brother's girlfriend stayed behind to watch Lilias. There was no way she was putting her granddaughter in a car with that man. Rather than bring Willow right back home, Jerry turned the opposite way when leaving the storage unit and drove to a house in the woods. Willow had no way of getting home, and since they had driven there in the dark she had no idea where she actually was. "I *know* I done wrong. I fucked up. I know it. But *please* let me explain!"

"God, you're pathetic." With that, Sunny hung up the phone. She and Willow didn't speak for over two years.

Morning turned into afternoon. Afternoon turned into evening. Evening turned into night. There was no sign of Willow. Sunny had driven through town, checked all the local bars, called the nearest hospitals, and even tried to remember where that old druggie shack had been up in the mountains. She was surprised to actually find it, or at least the remains of where it had once stood. Sunny had all but given up. She stayed at the farm that night and headed to Knoxville the following morning, but there was no sign of Willow there either. Sunny returned to the farmhouse defeated and utterly exhausted from worry. She tried to calm her mind by cleaning the house. Not that it was messy, but it seemed her grandfather hadn't dusted anything or swept the floors in months, if not years. There was something so satisfying to her whenever she cleaned. It didn't matter if it was her apartment, her desk at the office, or the dishes. Anything but laundry made her happy. She had never tried to describe it for fear of sounding crazy, but it was almost as if she felt total zen while cleaning.

Sunny swept the floors of the main level of the house, making her way from room to room. She finally arrived in the sitting room and decided that the stairs could wait. Leaning the broom against the wall, she sat down on the bench at the piano. She lightly ran her fingers across the keys without making a sound. Her mind drifted back to her childhood, and she could hear the hauntingly slow rendition of *Over the Rainbow* that her grandmother would play. Violet had learned it from her own mother, Cora. Not long after Violet's father left, *The Wizard of Oz* came out in theaters. Wanting to provide her young daughter with a bit of happiness, Cora splurged and bought movie theatre tickets. The song took hold of her and she began singing it around the house. Whenever she or Violet felt sad or they were going through hard times, they would sing that song to get them through. Violet played her own melancholic version along with many other beautiful songs, but Sunny now realized she very rarely played the piano when Howard was home.

Allowing her fingers to find the perfect place to rest, she sat up straight and began playing the opening to *Für Elise*. It was the only real piece of music Violet had taught her, and she would play as many notes as she could remember anytime she was near a piano. She wished she had just one more day with her grandmother so that she could finally learn *Over the Rainbow*. Of course, there were now multiple reasons she wished for more time with Violet.

As she continued playing, determined to get through without missing a note, Sunny didn't notice the house phone ringing. To be fair, she didn't realize the house phone was still in service. Once she heard it and realized what it was, she ran to the living room and answered the old rotary phone.

"Hello?"

"Uh, hey. Who's this?" a gruff voice responded.

"What do you mean, '*who's this*'? You called me, dude."

"Holy shit. Is that you, Sunny?"

Sunny was cautious as she answered. "Yeah, I'm Sunny. Who're you?"

"It's Brian. God I never expected you to answer at the farm."

Sunny relaxed and smiled. She hadn't talked to her step-father since the awful night of her fifteenth birthday. "Oh my God, Brian! How are you?" She had never felt anger toward him for leaving, because she couldn't blame him after what Willow had put him through.

"As much as I wish this could be a nice conversation to catch up with you, you gotta come get her."

"She's with you?! Where are you, Brian? I'll leave right now." That's when Sunny looked at the clock. In the midst of her therapeutic cleaning and impromptu piano recital, she hadn't realized it was nearly two o'clock in the morning. "Jesus, is that clock right?!" she asked under her breath.

Brian gave her his address which was in Johnson City. Sunny showed up at a small rancher-style home quarter-to-three. Before she could ring the bell, Brian opened the door.

"You gotta get her outta here. My wife's madder'n a bull backed into a hornets' nest."

Sunny grinned. "Congrats on getting married again!"

"Read the room, Sun! I ain't called you here for a goddamn reunion!"

"You're right. Sorry." Realizing she was deliriously tired, she focused on the matter at hand. "Where is she?" He pointed her toward the living room where Willow was on the couch. Aside from moving around a bit and letting out the occasional moan, she was mostly unconscious. "Christ. Any idea what she's on? I mean, do I need to take her to the hospital?"

"Naw. From what she told me when she showed up, she just been drinkin'. I called the folk she said she was with, and they said the same. She mentioned somethin' about mushrooms, but they didn't see her with nothing like that." Brian kept looking back at the hallway, anxious that his wife would make an unpleasant appearance.

"Oh, I was with her for the mushrooms," Sunny replied.

"Here I thought you had better sense than that. Shoulda known you'd end up just like her. Probably get lots of fancy drugs up there in New York, huh?"

"Okay, calm down. They were…uhh… medicinal mushrooms. Can you just help me get her in the car? You know, for old time's sake?" The feeling of déjà vu was thick in the room for both Brian and Sunny.

After they got her in the car, Sunny walked back to the front door with him. "Thanks for calling the farm, Brian. Honestly. I really do appreciate it."

"Next time I'm callin' the police. This shit ain't funny anymore. She needs help, Sun. Hell, I don't know. Maybe she's too far gone. You should just stay up there in New York. You never needed her anyhow. You's always better off without her."

Sunny smiled. "Thanks, Brian. You know, you were the closest thing I ever had to a real dad. I mean, it was only for a couple years, but I'll never forget you."

"Sunny, it's three o'clock in the goddamn mornin'. You got somethin' nice to say, say it in a letter or call me at a decent hour. Remember, next time she shows up here I'm callin' the cops." Brian walked into his house and as he closed the door he said, "Bullshit is what this is. Just bullshit." Sunny walked away from the porch, hearing Brian arguing with his wife from inside the house.

The smell of the freshly brewed coffee filled the kitchen. Sunny sat at the table, patiently waiting for Willow to wake up. She'd not made the same mistake of sleeping in separate rooms this time. Once they arrived back at the farm and Sunny had miraculously gotten Willow into the house and up the stairs, she didn't leave her side all night. If she'd had handcuffs, she would have bound herself to her mother to prevent another escape. She wasn't angry. She was relieved to find her mother in one piece, and to discover she had only been drinking was a victory in and of itself.

As soon as Sunny heard Willow coming down the stairs, she poured a cup of coffee and placed it across the table from her. Willow entered the room with her head hung low. She sat down and began drinking her coffee. They sat silently for nearly half an hour. It was not an uncomfortable silence, but rather one of safety and tolerance.

Once she finished her coffee, Willow stood up and began walking out of the room. She looked back at Sunny and motioned for her to follow. Without hesitation, Sunny jumped up from her seat and was quickly by her mother's side in the study. She remembered what Maisy had said about not asking questions, so she stayed quiet and waited for Willow to speak.

"She'd hide me in here. Mama would tell me it was a game, but it was how she'd hide me from him. There was heather in all the vases around the room." She took a deep breath and walked around the desk to the record player. She held the old record in her hands and said, "*Oh My Darlin, Clementine* on repeat." Willow began humming the tune as she looked out the window. "I seen it all happenin' again while I's trippin'."

She paused and Sunny walked around to be closer to her. Sunny could tell this was incredibly difficult for her mother, even though she had no idea what Willow had seen during her trip. "It's okay, mom. I'm here with you now."

"I didn't want to believe it, Sun. I didn't—" She couldn't finish her thought and began to cry, shaking her head and lightly pushing Sunny away when she tried to console her. Sunny backed off. The last thing she wanted was for her mom to shut down at such a critical moment. She watched intently as Willow leaned down in the corner of the room and pulled open the secret door.

"What the—" Sunny started to ask, but cut herself off.

Willow collapsed to a seated position in the corner next to the hidden nook, leaning her head against the wall. Sunny knelt down and looked inside. Underneath nearly fifty years of dust and cobwebs, she saw a crumpled blanket, a silver flashlight, and a stuffed mouse made from polka dot fabric. She looked back at her mother, still not understanding.

"She'd put me in here when he'd beat her. *'Into the mouse's house!'*" she said, mimicking her mother. "She never let him get too close to me when he was in a bad way. All the times I thought she was unfair, it was him. All the little things that kids never notice about grownups? I remember it now. That's what I's seein' in that trip. I could hear 'em fightin' after I'd gone to bed or when I's out in the yard. He was no good, Sun. The man I thought raised the sun each morning was a complete lie. How could I have blocked all that out?" She began trembling as Sunny held her hands. *"Why would she stay with him?"* she cried out.

Sunny sat next to her mother and held her while she wept. She then listened for nearly an hour as Willow recounted each part of her vivid trip into the past. Sunny was shocked. Maisy had mentioned that Howard had a jealous streak, but she never mentioned the types of abuse Willow was describing.

"I want to show you something, mom. Up in mamaw's room." Willow followed Sunny upstairs and into Violet's closet. "Look here. These two boxes, one's yours and one's mine."

Willow opened the box with her name on it. "What? What is all this?"

"It's like she saved everything from our childhoods. Every paper from school. Every drawing on a scrap piece of paper. Every… just everything."

"All this time. All this time and I never knew she cared about me at all. Why would she save all this if she didn't care?"

Sunny knew her mother was having a breakthrough, whether she realized it or not. "She *did* care for you, mom. To be honest, I think we were what she cared about most."

They decided to spend the remainder of the day resting and looking through the boxes of old book reports and long-lost diaries. They shared a lot of laughs as they read the papers aloud to each other. At the bottom of Willow's box, she discovered a thick envelope with no markings on the outside. She pulled out a dozen hand-written letters and began reading one to herself as Sunny sat quietly reading one of her elementary school journals.

"Uhh, Sun? You gotta see this," Willow said, handing her one of the letters.

Sunny's eyes darted from left to right as she scanned the letter. "A love letter?! Wait, who's Billy?"

"No idea. Looks like mama might've been gettin' some action on the side. Ain't no dates on any of these though. Ugh. Can you believe how he starts these letters? '*To the prettiest rose I know...*' Gross." Willow rolled her eyes at how corny it sounded.

"The code!" Sunny shouted as she stood up and hurried out of the room.

"The what? Hey, Sun! What the hell?" Willow yelled after her.

"Stay right there! I need to get something!" Sunny was already halfway down the stairs. A few moments later she returned with the stack of letters from the safety deposit box and the list of flowers Maisy had given her. "It's a code! See? Roses mean love!"

"It was also her last name, you ding-dong. Everything don't have to be a big mystery for you to solve."

"But these other letters! They're from Maisy when mamaw and grampa had already gotten married. She said it had to be written in code because grampa would be furious if he found out. So I bet she sent them *for* Billy as an extra layer of secrecy!"

"That seems like a bit of a stretch, Sun. Even for you." She knew there was no reasoning with her daughter once she became excited about an idea like this. It was strange for Willow to think of her mother as being in love with another man, but her curiosity was getting the better of her. Now that she knew the truth about her father, she began hoping Violet *did* have someone who loved her and cared for her.

The following morning, Willow and Sunny decided another visit into the mountains was necessary. Maisy and Theora were waiting for them.

Shortly after she finished her morning cup of coffee, Maisy saw Sunny's car pulling up, so she answered the door with her shoes and sweater already on. Willow wasted no time stopping at Maisy's house. Instead she bypassed it completely and went straight to the trail headed for Theora's shack. Maisy and Sunny hurried to catch up to her. She was no longer upset. She simply wanted answers, and she assumed she'd find the answers with Theora.

They found Theora in her rocking chair snoring loudly. Maisy woke her up, letting her know her company had arrived.

"The willow and the sunflower have returned so soon?" she asked.

Willow responded, "Yeah, we're back. And that tea you made me? Holy hell, Theora. You's right when you said it was unlike any other mushroom trip."

Theora simply smiled and said, "I'm glad you came back to see me."

Maisy, Sunny, and Willow took their seats just as they had at their previous meeting. The air in the room felt different this time.

Before there had been tension, mostly from Willow. Now it was much more welcoming and receptive.

"Can I get either of you something to drink?" Maisy asked while fixing herself and Theora a cup of tea.

"Hard pass," Willow was quick to respond. The three other women chuckled, relieved that the tone of the conversation was starting off so light-heartedly.

Once everyone was settled, Maisy asked, "How can we help you, Willow?"

She took a deep breath and looked down, shaking her head while wringing her hands together. Willow was desperately trying to hold it together. She despised crying in front of other people, and when she felt tears welling up in her eyes she would get angry, which would cause additional tears to form. It was a vicious cycle that she'd never been able to avoid once it started. Maisy, Theora, and Sunny all waited patiently and compassionately.

Without raising her head, Willow finally asked through a broken voice, "Why would she stay? *Why?* I just don't understand."

Maisy nodded her head. "That is a fair question, Willow. I often asked her the same thing all those years ago. The truth is, she was terrified of him. He had complete control over her from the beginning."

Willow looked up at her, confused. "Why didn't you convince her to leave? If you were such good friends, why didn't you help her?"

"I tried, my dear. Many times. It broke my heart more than you will ever know." It was obvious from the pain in her voice that Maisy had been tortured by these truths for most of her life.

Willow shook her head again, still finding it hard to believe that something couldn't have been done. Sunny sat silently, not knowing how or if she fit into this conversation. Theora simply rocked in her chair, using her dragon-adorned cane to propel herself. The room was quiet for several minutes. Since nobody was speaking, Sunny took it upon herself to push the conversation forward. Reaching into her purse, she pulled out the letters that had been locked away in the safety deposit box along with the letters from Billy.

"Maisy, we found these letters yesterday from someone named Billy. And I brought these that we found at the bank. Who is he? Is he why you wrote to her in code? I'm still trying to put all these pieces together." She handed the letters over to her. It was then that Theora noticed the ring on Sunny's hand and gasped.

"*Mother's ring!*" she said, reaching for Sunny's hand. Sunny, looking somewhat surprised, redirected her hand toward Theora so she could better see it. "Oh, I haven't seen this since I was a child. Did you know this is called a 'Rose of Sharon' ring? I would put it on when I was little and pretend to be a princess." Theora giggled like a child, and for a moment they could all picture her as the little girl she had once been.

Willow was confused. "Hold up. Why did *my* mama's bank box have *your* mama's ring?"

Maisy answered for Theora. "The ring belonged to my grandmother, who was Theora's mother. It was her engagement ring. She left it to me when she passed. I gave it to Violet many years ago." Maisy was shuffling through the letters.

"Why would you give my grandmother a family heirloom like that? Seems like something you'd want to keep or pass down to your own children." As she spoke, Sunny realized she had no idea if Maisy had a family beyond Theora.

Maisy did not answer except to say, "Oh I never did have children, dear."

Sunny lowered her head, embarrassed. "Oh, sorry. Umm, so who is this Billy guy?"

"Oh yes, Billy… Well, he was head over heels for Violet. And she was smitten with him. They started going together when we were just kids in school. They stayed together for many years, but they drifted apart. It's quite complicated." An awkward silence followed.

Theora finally spoke to Maisy. "Take them with you. *Show* them what you know to be true. It's the only way."

Sunny and Willow looked at each other and then to Maisy. She was looking into the fireplace, but her gaze was distant. Eventually, she nodded in agreement.

"Wait, what's happening? Where are you taking us?" Sunny asked as Theora stood up and began gathering jars from the shelves.

Theora said, "There is a small modification I can make to the reliving tea. Feng Chen warned that it is only to be used as a last resort in dire situations. In this tea, the three of you will all experience the same trip. You will see what Maisy has seen."

"How is that even possible?" Sunny asked. She was suddenly nervous about drinking the tea, but even more so about her mother going through the experience again.

"You mustn't ask questions like that. Mostly because I don't know how it is possible. Feng Chen did not explain *how* the tea works. You simply have to trust the process and be open to the experience."

Maisy had left the room to get the mushrooms from the cellar. Sunny and Willow looked at each other and began wordlessly conversing about how to proceed. Should they drink it? Should they politely decline? Should they simply run toward the car and not look back? Before they could come up with an answer, Maisy returned with the mushrooms.

"Hold on," Sunny said. "I thought you couldn't drink the reliving tea more than once without going crazy. That's what you said last time we were here."

"Oh you can relive as many times as you want, but you mustn't visit the same moment twice," Theora said as she made her way to the table.

"Ah, I see. That totally makes sense," Sunny said as she looked at Willow and shrugged.

They sat around the table watching Theora blend the ingredients as the water began boiling over the fire.

"Don't forget the sassafras!" Willow joked, causing Theora to snicker.

"Now," Theora said, pulling out a small dagger, "I'll need a drop of blood from each of you."

"Whoa! What the hell?!" Sunny exclaimed. "Nobody said we were going to cut ourselves!"

Theora gave her a puzzling look. "How else do you expect to be bound together on this trip?"

Maisy took the dagger and pricked the end of her index finger. After two or three drops of blood fell into the mortar with the other crushed ingredients, she wiped the dagger off with a small towel and passed it to Sunny. With the other women looking at her and going against every instinct in her body and mind, Sunny took the dagger to the end of her index finger just as Maisy had. She added her blood to the mixture and handed the dagger to Willow, who followed suit. Theora added the contents of the mortar to the boiling water and they waited for five minutes while it brewed. She ladled out three cups and passed them to each woman at the table.

"Once you have all finished the tea, Willow and Sunny will need to clear their minds completely. You are only along for the ride. Maisy will meditate on the memories she wishes for you to observe. As long as you are open to the journey, it will be successful." Theora stood up and made her way back to her rocking chair.

"Do you both understand?" Maisy asked as she picked up her cup.

Willow said, "Yeah I get it, but let me ask you this. When I's trippin' it was really, umm... Oh, what's the word? Disorienting? Or maybe disorganized? Like I'd hear all these sounds and start seein' different things and it was all chaotic and mixed up. I's afraid I'd get lost in it but I'd eventually figure it out. Is it gonna be like that? 'Cause if I'm bein' honest I don't never wanna experience that again."

"My memories will be a bit more clear. You see, you spent years *forgetting* but I've spent years *remembering*, unable to escape it. Haunted by it, day after day. Some of these memories were passed to me by this very method from Violet, and I can't ever forget them no matter how hard I've tried. If you want to know the truth, this is the only way." There was an anguish in her comments that was unsettling to Sunny. "Are we ready?"

Willow and Sunny looked at each other and then back at Maisy and nodded. The three women then drank the tea without conversing any further. Once they had finished, Willow and Sunny sat together on the cot where Willow's first trip had taken place. Maisy stayed in her seat at the table.

"Don't you need to lie down?" Sunny asked.

With a sly grin Maisy said, "Oh sweet Sunny, this isn't my first cup of tea." She winked at them before closing her eyes to begin her meditation. Sunny and Willow looked at each other and held hands, as they too closed their eyes and prepared for the trip.

Young girls giggling. . . . . bare feet splashing in a creek. . . . .
"I'll tie him across the railroad tracks!". . . . . sun shining against
warm skin. . . . . a toad hops into tall grass. . . . . small hands picking
raspberries. . . . . lightning bugs twinkling in the dark. . . . .

The calendar on the wall of the kitchen reads "July 1943". The
newspaper on the counter describes the ongoing Allied invasion of
Sicily. Eight-year-old Violet is sitting at the table with her mother
eating breakfast. She eats her fried egg and biscuit quickly, eager to
start her day. After washing her plate and glass in the sink, she grabs
a bucket near the door, kisses her mother, and heads outside.

In the distance down the dirt road, young Maisy runs toward
Violet carrying her own bucket. As the girls meet up on the edge of a
field, they lock arms and begin skipping barefoot along the fenceline
while singing,

> *"Pa bought a big ol' billy goat,*
> *And ma she washed most every day!*
> *Hung her clothes out on the line,*
> *But that goat he changed her mind!*

Tore down the ol' red flannel.
Shoulda heard those buttons crack!
'I'll get even with the son-of-a-gun.
I'll tie him across the railroad track!'
Tied him across the railroad tracks,
And the train was comin' at a powerful rate!
He belched up that ol' red shirt,
And he flagged down that darned ol' freight!"

The girls giggle as they finish their song and arrive at their destination. The raspberries are ripe and ready to be picked. They fill their bellies before filling their buckets as their laughter, silliness, and innocence fills the hollow. The horrors across the ocean and the hardships across the country are not a burden they must bear. They are completely free and full of joy and innocence. They feel the world is perfect and complete as long as they are together.

The girls, now sun-kissed and sweaty, return the berry-filled buckets to Cora who is busy mending dresses. She tells them to go cool themselves off before starting the afternoon chores, and they gladly oblige. Hand in hand, they run through the small field of wildflowers to the shade of the trees lining the creek. The girls each strip down to their undergarments before wading into the cool water. They search for tadpoles and small fish. They have stick races in the slow moving water. Eventually, they climb onto the banks and lay next to each other listening to the birds singing in the trees.

Maisy asks, "Do you think we'll always be friends and play together?"

Violet looks at her, confused. "Why wouldn't we? We're like sisters."

"Well, my mama hasn't seen her sister in a real long time."

"That's because your mama's sister went across the ocean all them years ago. I ain't goin' anywhere. Are you?"

Maisy laughs. "No way! I just want to stay with you forever. Let's promise to always be best friends." The girls shake hands before Maisy adds, "Actually, my mama's sister is moving back here. We got a letter from her last week sayin' she's comin' in a month or so. I sure hope she's nice."

"Yeah, me too. Maybe she'll bring you a present from over there. Where is it that she lives?"

"Umm, Vietnam? It's about a hundred miles away from here, I think. It's *really* far."

"Oh, wow. I hope she has pictures of what it looks like!" The girls rest silently on the banks of the creek for a few moments longer before Violet says, "We should probably get back to the house. Mama'll have my neck if I don't get a bushel of beans picked."

The girls stand up and brush off the dirt as best they can from their now mostly dry undergarments. They put their clothes on and begin the journey back to the farmhouse, straying from the path only to chase a toad until they lose him in the tall grass. Upon returning home, they pick green beans, clean out the chicken coop, and bring in the dry clothes from the line. As the sun fades behind the trees on the mountainous horizon, Cora sits on the porch watching the two girls chase lightning bugs in the yard. Violet and Maisy embrace tightly before Maisy takes off down the dirt road toward her own house. She looks back several times, and Violet never turns away until her friend is completely out of sight.

A nervous and excited feeling. . . . . crickets chirping in the dark. . . . . the popping and crackling of a record player. . . . . cold water on sore feet. . . . . a bashful smile. . . . .

The calendar on the wall of the kitchen reads "July 1950". The newspaper on the counter details the first days of the Korean War. Fifteen-year-old Violet enters the room wearing the dress Cora has made for her. It is sleeveless, black with white polka-dots and red trim. It is tight around the waist, and the skirt is wide and flared. She is absolutely glowing. Cora smiles in disbelief. Her little girl has become a young woman. Violet kisses her mother on the cheek before practically floating out of the house and into the passenger's seat of the car. Cora drives her into town to the First Baptist Church where a sign out front advertises the Summer Sock-Hop. Maisy, wearing a yellow dress with a white checked pattern, is standing near the door waiting for Violet. The girls embrace and compliment each other's dresses before waving to Cora and entering the church.

The room is divided with girls on one side and boys on the other. Adult chaperones are scattered about, talking amongst themselves. The music on the record player, which was meticulously vetted by the church elders, is a mix of bluegrass, classical, and gospel. Violet and Maisy walk across the room together. They giggle as they look over at the group of boys.

"Do you think you'll dance with anyone tonight?" Maisy asks.

"Oh gosh. I don't know. Do you think any of them would dance with me? I mean, I guess if someone asks me I'll say yes." Violet blushes at the thought of a boy asking her to dance. All the kids in attendance had grown up together, but this was the first time they were in a situation with a romantic overtone.

"I'm surprised Billy hasn't already asked you! You two seem quite friendly lately," she teases. "But by the looks of this room I'm not sure anyone is going to dance tonight. It's like they're afraid of us." Both girls laugh. Maisy extends her hand out to Violet while bowing down and asks, "My dearest darling Violet, would you do me the honor of dancing with me on this lovely evening?"

Violet can't contain her laughter as she takes Maisy's hand. They walk into the center of the dance floor and begin dancing together. Twirling each other and twisting so that their skirts fan out around them. Their smiles are lighting up the room, and their joy is contagious. The other girls quickly join in. The boys watch, still nervous but gradually building up their confidence. Finally one brave boy wanders out on a dare, like a canary into a mine. A girl grabs his hand and they begin dancing together. That's all the proof the other boys need. Everyone is now on the dance floor.

The song changes. The tempo is much slower, and the boys and girls begin pairing off. A young boy named Stanley asks Maisy to dance, while Billy asks Violet. For the rest of the evening, they remain paired up with these boys. It is the first time Violet has thought about the possibility of having a *real* boyfriend. She and Billy have been close friends in school, and she has always found him handsome. In the church basement with one of his arms around her waist and another holding her hand, she has an entirely new feeling. It is powerful, and she wants to feel more.

Cora drives the girls back to the farmhouse after the dance is over. She heads inside, but the girls kick their shoes off onto the porch and decide to walk to the creek. The air is humid and the temperature is hot. They are both sticky with sweat from the hours of dancing and the cold water of the creek is calling them.

On the bank they begin removing their dresses and petticoats. They find a deeper part of the creek that will cover more than just their aching feet. Wading in up to their waists, the cold water momentarily takes their breath away causing them to laugh. Once the initial shock wears off, the cold water feels refreshing. They splash around while talking about the events of the evening, such as favorite songs, least favorite chaperones, and funniest moments.

"How was it dancing with Billy? Are you in love?" Maisy asks with a giggle.

Violet splashes water at her. "No, I am not!"

"Oh come on! You two were all over each other on the dance floor!"

"I know. He's just... oh, he's just so dreamy." She smiles and twirls in the water as she says this. "Do you really think he likes me?" Violet is nervous asking the question for fear that Maisy might say no.

"Of course he likes you! You'd have to be blind not to see that. Good grief!"

Satisfied with that response, Violet changes the subject before they discuss it any further. "Well what about you and Stanley? You two were inseparable all night!"

Maisy scrunches her nose. "Stanley?! Ugh. He's such a cold fish. Stepped on my feet so many times and never said one interesting thing the whole night. Didn't even tell me I looked pretty!"

Violet laughs at Maisy's outburst. The girls are silent for a few minutes and the only sound filling the air is the chirp of the crickets and the rippling water. The lightning bugs glow in the canopy of trees overhead. Maisy sits on a large stone in the middle of the creek and lets the water rush over her feet. Violet stands next to her, leaning against the rock in water up to her knees.

"Can I ask you something, Vi?"

"Anything, you know that," Violet responds.

"Did Billy... you know... kiss you?" Maisy stumbles over the words, unsure how to ask without embarrassing herself.

"No way!" Violet replies quickly. "Are you crazy?! I wouldn't kiss a boy in the church basement! That'd give the chaperones a heart attack!" They laugh at the idea of the church biddies fussing over a teenage love story unfolding in the Sunday school classrooms.

Maisy's nerves have never been higher. She finally asks, "Have you *ever* kissed a boy?"

Violet lowers her head and looks at the water. "No," she says quietly. She's ashamed. She knows other girls her age have kissed a boy by now. "Have you?" she asks.

Maisy shakes her head. "I wouldn't even know how." There's an electricity building in the air that they both feel. "Maybe *we* could…" She shrugs her shoulders as they look into each other's eyes.

Violet nods slightly and says, "Okay." The feeling she had while dancing with Billy has returned. This time it's even more powerful. This time she feels safe because she's with Maisy.

She steps in front of Maisy who is still sitting on the stone. They lean closer and close their eyes as their lips meet. Maisy wraps her arms around Violet's waist, and Violet's hands move to Maisy's shoulders. After several seconds that feel like a blissful eternity, the girls smile at each other and bashfully look away.

"Well, I guess now we both know how it's done. Doesn't seem as scary anymore, huh?" Maisy said, breaking the awkward silence.

"Not scary at all," Violet said with a slight giggle. "We should probably get back to the house. Mama'll start worryin' if we don't."

At the farmhouse the girls are laying in the large canopy bed. As they begin to fall asleep Maisy says, "Promise we'll always be together."

"Always, Maisy. Always."

"And Vi, if you ever want to practice… you know… again, I'd be okay with that."

Violet is quiet except for her heartbeat that she fears is loud enough to wake her mother in the next room. "I— I'd be okay with that."

Both girls smile as they drift off to sleep.

A flickering light. . . . . a feeling of pure happiness. . . . . a clap of thunder. . . . . a golden rose. . . . . sweet raspberries. . . . . a rusted tractor. . . . .

The calendar on the wall of the kitchen reads "July 1955". The newspaper on the counter describes a new park that will open soon in California called *Disneyland*. Twenty-year-old Violet is washing the dishes. She is dressed in a waitressing uniform. Cora enters the room with the assistance of a cane.

"Oh no, mama. Is the rheumatism actin' up again?" Violet asks, drying her hands on her apron.

"Oh just a touch. Not anything to concern yourself with. A little stiff this mornin', that's all. You goin' in for lunch?" she asks as she sits down at the table.

Violet pours her a cup of coffee. "Yes, ma'am. Me and Maisy are gonna go pick some berries for you once we're done if it don't storm this afternoon. I think there's enough for several quarts of jam and maybe a few cobblers."

"Oh that would be nice. Supposed to be a hot one today."

"Want me to make you some breakfast before I go?" Violet asks.

Cora waves her off. "Don't fuss over me. I'm alright. Just bring me some berries and try not to eat 'em all. I probably lost a hundred quarts of jam to you two stealin' my berries over the years." She smiles at her daughter. She knows it's only a matter of time before she'll be getting married and making her own life.

"What?! Oh mama, we would never!" Violet grins and kisses her mother on the forehead before walking out of the house.

The diner is nearly empty. The lunch rush has cleared out and while Violet wipes down the tables Maisy dances around the dining room with a broom as the jukebox plays *Only You* by The Platters.

Maisy sweeps up next to the table where Violet is cleaning and speaks into the end of the broom as if it were a microphone. "Now tell me, Miss Rose. Who was it that sat at this here table less than one hour ago?"

Violet rolls her eyes. She whispers, "You know damn well who sat here."

"Ah yes, but I want to hear *you* say the name. Can you tell us? All of our listeners are just *dying* to hear!" She leans the pretend microphone toward Violet and smiles.

Deciding to play along, Violet sighs and speaks into the broom handle. "Mr. Howard Richmond."

Maisy squeals with delight. "Oh do tell! Is this man a *friend* of yours? Hmm?"

"Maybe," she replies with a sheepish grin. "Now hurry up and sweep, please. Mama's expectin' a whole mess of berries this afternoon." Violet snaps her towel and hits Maisy's hip, causing her to jump and playfully grab at Violet's arm. They share a smile and a knowing gaze.

At the berry patch the buckets are half full. Storm clouds are forming in the distance, but they know they still have at least another hour before it hits. Maisy is nervous, but not because of the distant thunder. Something is eating away at her mind and she isn't sure how to talk about it. She decides to be direct.

"Do you think he'll ask you to marry him?" Her eyes don't leave the brambles as she speaks.

Violet stops. "I'm not sure. Maybe."

"Will you say yes if he does?"

She considers it for a moment before resuming her berry picking. "Perhaps. I mean, he's well off and quite popular in town. I think he could really make something of himself. He has such grand plans for the future. And I expect he'd be a good father and able to provide for a family." She essentially talks herself into it by adding, "Yes, now that I really think about it I suppose I would say yes to him if he proposed. It's wild to think about, but I'm not getting any younger and I don't hardly ever hear from Billy since he left for college. I thought for sure he was the one, but it doesn't make sense to keep waitin' for him. He says it'll be somethin' like seven more years of school to get his law degree! Besides, he won't want to marry a simple country girl like me. I'm sure he's meetin' lots of smart, successful girls. So yeah, Howard might actually be the one."

Maisy is silent for a moment before saying, "That's really exciting. I'm very happy for you, Vi. Truly." There is a sadness in her voice that is impossible to conceal.

"You'll find someone soon, Maisy. I'm sure of it! And then we'll grow old together, raising our babies while our husbands drink beer and play gin on the dining room table."

Maisy forces a smile and realizes her bucket is now full. "You about done over there? My bucket's about to spill out."

"Yep, I'm full. Want to head to the creek? We can probably cool off and make it back before the storm blows in."

Just as they had been doing every summer since they were kids, the women strip down to their underwear and wade into the creek, playfully splashing each other. Sensing her heartache, Violet grabs Maisy's hand and pulls her in close. She wraps Maisy's arms around her hips and places her arms around Maisy's neck.

"I'm not going anywhere, Maisy. I'll still be here with you."

Maisy fights back tears. "It won't be the same, Vi. It just won't be."

Violet rests her head on Maisy's shoulder and lightly kisses her neck. The women hold their embrace, gently swaying back and forth in a silent dance, as Maisy begins to cry.

A loud clap of thunder startles the women. Beneath the trees lining the creek they are unable to see that the weather has deteriorated. Realizing they have misjudged the speed of the approaching storm, they race out of the creek, grabbing their clothes and berry buckets. The wind is blowing hard and the rain stings as it hits their bare skin. Violet grabs Maisy's hand and pulls her off the path and toward the old pole barn. She knows it is the closest structure where they can safely ride out the storm.

The barn is dark inside, but Violet quickly finds an old oil lamp and a matchbook on the workbench. Once lit, they begin looking around the large structure. A rat scurries away from the light and into a dark corner. Cobwebs cover an old rusted tractor. The air is hot and thick, as only a slight breeze from the storm enters through the cracks of the barn walls. Maisy finds an old blanket on a shelf and pulls it down. It is covered in oil stains from years of laying beneath a tractor undergoing maintenance. Together they shake off the dust and lay it across some old, busted hay bales. Leaning against an old tractor tire, they sit close together and listen to the rain pounding against the tin roof of the barn while snacking on berries.

"How're you feeling?" Violet asks.

Maisy only shrugs. Water drips from the end of her hair, lands on her arm, and slides down her warm skin.

Violet frowns. "I hate that you're upset with me. I hate that I'm hurting you, Maisy. You have to understand that's not at all what I want."

Maisy sits up and turns to face her. "What do you want, Vi? I mean, what do you *really* want? Because I sure as hell can't figure it out."

Violet is startled by her tone. "I don't understand. I just—"

"You say we'll always be together. And when we're alone and in each other's arms I'm the happiest I've ever been. But then you start spending all this time with Howard. So much so that you're considering *marrying* him and talking about what a great father he'll be! But where does that leave me? Huh?! I'll tell you. It leaves me alone. I'm in love with you and yet I'm completely alone." It is the first time Maisy has had the nerve to stand up for herself and speak freely about her feelings toward Violet.

Violet sits up a little straighter. "You're... you're in love with me?"

Maisy lowers her head. "Of course I am. I always have been."

Violet holds her hand and says, "I think I'm in love with you too, Maisy. I didn't realize that's what I was feeling until just now hearing you say it. But it's true. I love you." They both begin to smile.

"I want to give you something," Maisy says. She stands up and walks to their pile of clothing and gets a small velvet pouch from the pocket of her skirt. She sits back down and pulls out the Rose of Sharon ring. "This was my grandmother's ring. She gave it to my mama, and my mama gave it to me. I want you to have it, Vi. I can't ever imagine loving another person the way I love you. You're the most important person in the world to me." She slides the ring onto Violet's finger.

"Oh, Maisy. It's so beautiful," she says as she admires the ring on her hand.

A tear slowly begins its journey down Violet's cheek. Maisy cradles her face in her hand, brushing the lone teardrop away. Their eyes meet. The urges they have felt in the past, no matter how forbidden, can no longer be suppressed. As the storm rages outside, the orange flickering light from the oil lamp casts their shadows against the weathered walls. The barn door has been left ajar and unbeknownst to Violet and Maisy a flash of lightning reveals Howard standing outside in the pouring rain. He watches as the two shadows become one, and malice begins pulsing through his veins.

A beam of sunlight. . . . . a harsh voice. . . . . a missing shirt button. . . . . a bouquet of flowers. . . . . a broken heart. . . . .

The calendar on the wall of the kitchen still reads "July 1955". Yesterday's newspaper about *Disneyland* is now lining the waste basket. Cora sits at the table drinking coffee as Violet walks in, still in her nightgown.

"Good morning, mama. Are you feelin' any better today?" she asks while she pours herself a glass of orange juice.

"Oh yes, I'm feeling much better. I suppose my rheumatism was actin' up on account of the weather. That storm was somethin' else. Where'd you and Maisy end up after pickin' berries?"

"We were in the creek coolin' off. I thought we had more time before it was gonna hit us, but it must have been movin' fast. We had to run to the old pole barn till it was over with." Her heart starts beating faster as she remembers it all so vividly.

"That Richmond boy, he come by here right before the storm blowed in. Brought you a pretty bunch of flowers, too." She points to a vase sitting on the windowsill with a bouquet of tulips.

Violet's heart drops and her eyes grow wide. "Howard was here? Yesterday? What did you tell him?"

"I told him you's out pickin' berries and that you'd be back 'fore the storm come in. He acted like he might go lookin' for you'ns, but I looked back out and his car was gone. Probably scared of the storm. Can you imagine?" She laughs and shakes her head in disapproval. "A *real* gentleman would have waited. Don't you forget that."

Violet nods her head, slightly panicked but unsure why.

"Did Maisy make it home okay after the storm?" She raises her eyebrows and looks over the rim of her glasses.

"Yes, mama. We forgot the berries in the pole barn though. I'll run out and get 'em after I finish eatin'."

Walking to the pole barn, Violet's mind is racing. She thinks about Maisy. She wonders why a feeling so beautiful could be thought of as wrong. She doesn't understand how she could be confused about something that felt so right. Her mind switches to

Howard. She wonders if it is possible to be in love with two people at the same time. After realizing she is in love with Maisy, she wonders if she would still say yes to a proposal from Howard. Before her mind is able to conjure up anymore thoughts, she hears a voice calling out to her.

"Violet! Wait up!" Howard shouts as he jogs up the trail behind her.

Violet gasps and her muscles contract. "Howard! Don't you dare sneak up on me like that again! You nearly gave me a heart attack!"

He chuckles as he catches up with her. He places his hand on her back and leans in, kissing her on the cheek. "I'm sorry, darlin'. I honestly didn't mean to startle you." He reaches down and picks a wildflower and hands it to her. "Forgive me?"

She smiles as she takes the flower from him. They walk down the path along the fenceline, hand-in-hand. Violet says, "Mama said you were at the house before the storm yesterday. I'm sorry I missed you."

"Oh, that's alright. I shoulda stayed longer, but when I saw how quickly that storm was movin' in I figured I should get over to my mother's home to bring in the wash before my briefs and undershirts were blown clear across the county!"

This makes Violet laugh as she walks into the pole barn. "I just need to grab these buckets to bring back to the house." Before she reaches them, Howard closes the barn door behind him and latches it, causing Violet to stop in her tracks.

Her heart sinks deep into her chest. With the door closed she feels trapped. She turns and looks at him, asking, "Why'd you close the door?" She tries to smile, but her fear is undeniable.

"I just want some alone time with my pretty girl. We been goin' steady for quite a while now, Violet." He walks closer to her. He sees the blanket still stretched out over the hay. He looks back at her, smiling in a way that frightens her. "I want to know you better."

She begins stumbling over her words. Her hands are shaking. "W-w-what do you mean? Y-y-you know me better than anyone, Howard. You can ask me anything. Anything, really. W-w-what do you want to know?"

He's standing close to her now. He rubs his hands up and down her arms. "I don't want to *ask* you anything." His grip on her arms tightens and she winces at the pain. "I want to know you the way that *whore* got to know you yesterday afternoon."

Before she has time to react, Howard throws her down on the blanket and is on top of her. She tries to crawl away but he grabs her shirt, ripping the buttons off and exposing her breasts. She starts to scream but his hand covers her mouth.

"*BE STILL!*" he whispers harshly into her ear, drops of his spit landing on her cheek.

She tries her hardest to fight and he struggles to hold her down. He is too strong though, and he easily overpowers her. She stops resisting. She notices a beam of sunlight shining through two planks of the barn wall. She focuses on the dust particles dancing through the air, passing in and out of the spotlight as they perform a reticent ballet for her. The world falls silent as the rhythmical pain, both physical and emotional, grows too strong for her. She tries one last time to cry out, but as she loses consciousness she only hears the harsh whisper. "*BE STILL!*"

The occasional creak from Theora's rocking chair along with the crackling of the fire were the only sounds filling the shack. It had been just over one hour since they began their trip. The three women's eyes suddenly opened wide as they intensely gasped for air.

"A simultaneous awakening. A successful journey indeed," Theora said while nodding her head with pride.

Though they were still holding hands, Sunny quickly grabbed Willow's arm with her free hand and pulled her closer as if she were a bashful child in a room full of strangers. If they had been standing she might have hid behind her completely. Once the three women caught their breath, Willow began moving toward the table. Sunny held on tight, never letting go of her mother. This was her first psychedelic trip of any kind and she had not been prepared for the intensity of what she experienced.

Without looking at anyone in particular Willow said, "So let me get this straight... Just tell me... I mean... I can't... What the fu—"

"It's all true. Every bit of it," Maisy replied.

"He *raped* her?! And she still married him after that? *Why?!* It doesn't make any sense!" Willow was shaking her head, desperate to understand.

Maisy sighed. "She came to me a few nights after and told me everything. Vi was so ashamed and scared. Howard acted as if nothing happened. Kept on treating her like they were still going steady and that everything was fine. But she had seen the evil in his eyes. And those words, '*be still*', those haunted her for the rest of her life. She knew he was not the man she thought he was, but by then it was too late. She was afraid to tell him it was over. So me and Vi, we talked about it a lot over the next few weeks and we decided we'd run away. We had a whole plan of how we would escape and where we would go." She picked up a pitcher and poured herself and her guests a glass of water. "We even had the date picked out that we were to leave."

Sunny finally spoke after taking a sip of water. "So where did you go?"

Maisy's faint smile was full of sadness. "We never left, dear. By then Violet realized she was pregnant."

Fearing she already knew the answer Willow quietly asked, "With me?"

Maisy nodded. Sunny covered her face with her hands.

"So that's why. That's why she didn't love me." The way she said it, so matter-of-factly while staring down at the table, was heartbreaking for Sunny. Willow continued, "I trapped her in that house with him. She didn't even want me and she couldn't—"

Maisy leaned forward and grabbed Willow's hands with a fierceness in her eyes and a sternness in her voice. "She wanted you more than anything in this world. Don't you *ever* doubt Violet's love for you, Willow."

Theora nodded. "It's true. The girls came to me wondering what to do and asked if I could help them. I know how to make a tea that could make the pregnancy stop, but she refused. She wanted the baby, wanted *you*, even though it meant that man would always be in her life."

"Oh please! If she liked babies so much why am I an only child?" Willow asked with a scoff.

"Well, that is my doing," Theora confessed.

Willow's eyes grew wide as she asked, "Did you... Did you tie her tubes?"

Theora and Maisy looked at each other and began laughing hysterically. "Could you imagine *me* performing a surgery?!" Theora asked.

"Oh, Lord. I'm not sure the last time I laughed this hard." Maisy wiped away a tear from her eye as her laughter finally died down. "Howard wanted more children, but your mother refused. Oh she made him think she wanted more, but Theora made her a sort of, umm—"

"Morning-after tea," Theora said.

Willow wondered how often her mother needed that tea, but she didn't dare ask.

"She still could have run away. Why didn't you stick with your plan?" Sunny asked.

"I told you. She was absolutely terrified of him. And once he found out about the baby, well they went straight to the courthouse and got married. Didn't even tell Miss Cora! She was absolutely distraught. Her only child getting married without her even knowing about it!" Maisy took another sip of water and began fanning herself with a newspaper.

"Wow. I mean, to think we lived our whole lives and never knew about any of this. I just... I just can't believe it." Sunny was shaking her head, still in shock over all that had been revealed.

Willow had a puzzled look on her face. "Hold up. Are we actually gonna skip over the fact that I just found out my mama was a dyke?!"

Sunny's eyes grew wide as she snapped, "*Mom! What the hell?!*" She turned to Maisy and added, "I'm so sorry. I can't even—"

Maisy nodded. "It's fine, Sunny."

Theora added, "Even *I* know that's inappropriate."

Willow became defensive. "What?! It's true! You said it was all true, right?"

Maisy said, "We never labeled our relationship. We were—"

"Lesbians," Willow said, cutting her off.

"*Christ*," Sunny whispered as she raised her hand to her forehead.

Maisy ignored Willow and continued, "—in love. Violet was the absolute love of my life. And I'd like to think I was the love of hers. I've never felt a connection to another human being like the one I felt with her. She was truly a part of me, as important as my arm or my leg. I never much cared for dating the boys we went to school with like Vi did. I was happy simply spending time with her. We kept it all a secret, but I think Miss Cora knew. She never let on though. She just wanted us to be happy. Everyone always said it was wrong, but we never really understood why."

"Because it ain't right, that's why," Willow said, but she was suddenly unsure of herself.

Theora lightly tapped her cane on the floor and said, "Love is rarely wrong."

"Havin' feelings like *that* is." Willow was unnerved. She realized she was spewing out arguments she'd heard from others over the course of her life. She wasn't actually sure how she truly felt.

"That is your first mistake. Love is not only a feeling," Theora responded in her soothing, hypnotic voice. "Love is an energy, a powerful force that is unable to be controlled or contained. Mothers love their babies before they are even born. We continue loving those we've lost long after they are gone. Love is always a part of us, whether we *feel* it or not. When those energies collide between two people in a way that leaves the universe a bit more harmonious, well, some call that soulmates. I believe that is what is meant by true love. And that energy, that universal power, *that* is rarely wrong."

Willow was looking down at her lap, unsure of how to reply. Normally she would argue, but she didn't feel right sassing Theora.

"Look at the two pictures hanging on the wall over there," Theora said, pointing to paintings she had brought back from Vietnam. "Which one speaks to you? If you had to choose one, which would you say you desire?"

Willow studied them and eventually said, "The one on the right."

"Why?" Theora asked.

Willow shrugged. "I don't know. I just prefer that one I guess."

"And I choose the one on the left. Does that make me wrong?"

"No," Willow said, shaking her head.

"Does it make me a bad person?" Theora asked.

"No."

"Does *my* desire affect *your* life in any way?"

Willow lowered her head again. "No, ma'am."

"And so it is the same with love. Love is rarely wrong." Theora said, tapping her cane on the floor once more to signal the matter was settled.

Following a brief, awkward silence Sunny continued, "So you gave my mamaw the ring that night in the barn. You said it was your grandma's engagement ring. Were *you* hoping to use it like an engagement ring?"

"An *engagement* ring?" Maisy chuckled at the absurdity of the question. "You realize this was back in the fifties, right? We were lucky to not get burned at the stake for such 'immoral' behavior. No, I didn't want to *marry* her. Marriage was so far out of reach for us back in those days there was no sense in even thinking about it. I just wanted her in my life. I wanted her to choose me. To love me. I was sure she wanted the same, so I gave her the ring as a way to show how serious my love for her truly was. The happiness that filled my heart whenever she was near," she paused and took a deep breath. "Well, it was a high unlike any drug can provide. We were together as much as any two people can be. It was as if our souls were braided together.

"After Vi told Howard about the pregnancy and they got married, I stopped by the house one afternoon. Miss Cora was the only one there and she was in an awful state. I could tell she'd been crying. She never did like Howard, and the fact that he was now her son-in-law just devastated her. She told me that day that he was going to put her in a nursing home. Told her it was too dangerous for her to go up and down those stairs each day with her rheumatism. I assured her there was no way Violet would allow it, but less than a week later she was gone. I visited her a few times, but she died just a year or so later. I think it simply broke her heart to be treated like that, kicked out of her childhood home, and she never recovered."

"How did he get away with all of this? I mean, didn't anyone else notice? Couldn't you go to the police?" Sunny asked.

Maisy shook her head. "He had the police wrapped around his finger. They were mostly old friends of his or of his father's. He was so well connected in town that nobody dared cross him. And once he became mayor, well, he was practically untouchable."

"I still don't understand why, especially once she had me, she'd stay with someone like him. You'd think she'd want to protect me from him." Willow's eyes were darting around the room as though she might find the answers hidden somewhere in Theora's shack.

"Yes, this was always a concern of mine as well. The truth is, he threatened her. Not that he would hurt *her*, no. He did that all the time. Howard told her on more than one occasion that if she left, he would hunt her down and harm *you*. He knew that was the only way she'd stay. She would protect you at all costs, no matter how badly *she* was treated. If it meant you were safe, she would endure anything," Maisy said.

Willow sat back and reflected on Maisy's statements. She couldn't help but feel responsible for the abuse her mother suffered all those years, but she also began feeling something new. Something she'd never felt toward her mother before. Gratitude. Respect. Sympathy. She was in uncharted waters, but unlike before these waters were calm and serene. The hostility and malevolence she held onto for so many years had transferred from her mother to her father. Willow wasn't sure how to deal with all of this. As she had so many times before, she hoped Sunny would have a plan for what to do next.

Sunny said, "I know I've wrongfully assumed multiple times that we know the whole story. Dare I ask? Is this it? I mean, do we know it all now or are there more bombshells you need to drop?"

"I think that's all of it, Sunny. Violet and I began our secret meetings almost as soon as Howard banished me from her life. I wrote her a letter and sent it to the house, but he happened to be the one who picked up the mail that day. That's when we set up the post office box and I began writing in code."

"Yes! The code! Can you tell us more about that? I guess I was wrong thinking that you were writing to her for Billy, huh?" Sunny couldn't wait to read through the letters again now that she was beginning to understand the relationship between Maisy and Violet.

"Of course! In these letters," she said lightly touching the stack of papers on the table, "whenever you see mention of roses, that is my love for her. Anemones symbolize the fact that our love was forbidden, and I think a few times I mentioned forget-me-nots which meant I was afraid she would move on and no longer need me. Of course, if you read anything about lavender or thistle or petunias or a recipe that calls for basil, well that's all directed toward Howard."

Sunny cocked her head to the side. "Wait... thistle and petunias?" she asked, rubbing her arm.

"Yes, dear. Thistle represents hatred and distrust. Petunias are for anger and resentment." Maisy winked at Sunny, realizing the anonymous flower arrangement she sent to the funeral home was no longer anonymous at all.

Maisy then talked with them at length about the garden Violet was so proud of. Willow and Sunny couldn't recall the specific flowers that had been planted there, but Maisy remembered them well. In addition to the letters she would send, Maisy would bring potted plants to each of their secret visits. She had been the one who provided the dogwood trees that had been planted near the garden. Willow thought about how upset Violet became when one of them was hit by lightning, and she always wondered why her mother would cry over a tree. Maisy explained that dogwoods represent love overcoming adversity, so when one of them was destroyed Violet couldn't help but see it as some sort of grim message from the universe. Of course, heather was planted all around the porch and within the garden for protection. Violet had the most beautiful rose bushes in the county, all of which had come from Maisy. Forget-me-nots were planted near the snowdrops, which symbolized hope. Rosemary, remembrance and wisdom, were side by side with the chamomile, providing strength to weather any storm. Willow and Sunny were fascinated by the description of the garden. They had no idea it was so meticulously designed and full of hidden meaning.

"The more you talk about it the more I'm remembering. Seems like there were massive ferns next to those wagon wheels. Do you remember that mom?" Sunny asked, looking at Willow.

Before she could respond Maisy said, "Oh yes. I brought her several ferns from just outside here." She pointed to the door of Theora's shack. "Ferns are a sign of secrecy. Obviously something quite important to our situation. Of course they can also refer to something magical."

"What about dandelions? What do they mean?" Sunny wasn't thinking about the garden anymore. She was actually wondering why there were so many growing near Theora's house.

Maisy smiled knowingly and said, "Fortune-telling. We figured a witch doctor like Theora should have a proper garden leading to her home."

Theora simply nodded her head, saying, "I'm not much of a gardener, but I can keep dandelions alive. They make excellent teas and salads. Plus I like to blow on them once they become fuzzy." She grinned her childlike grin.

It was late afternoon when Willow and Sunny decided they needed to get on the road. They were both exhausted from the day's events and knew that navigating the mountain roads was not something they wanted to try after dark. They thanked Theora for her hospitality and began walking the trail back toward Maisy's house. Once they arrived, they stood in Maisy's garden saying their goodbyes.

"I honestly don't know what to say, Miss Maisy," Sunny said.

"Nothing needs to be said, dear. As far as I'm concerned, I've fulfilled all my promises to Violet so I am completely at peace."

"Promises?" Willow asked.

"It was during one of our last secret visits. Of course, I don't know how secret they really were at that point. Howard didn't much care anymore so long as he didn't have to see me. I went to the farmhouse one afternoon when I knew he wouldn't be around. Violet and I walked back to the creek. I had to practically carry her because she was so weak by then. Oh we must have been a sight to see. Two old ladies stumbling down that overgrown trail. Anyone that saw us probably thought we were half lit." She laughed remembering the scene. "We sat on the bank with our feet in the water and talked about anything and everything. But she made me promise that I would tell you, both of you, the truth. *Her* truth. *Our* truth. That was an easy promise to make. The other was the hardest thing I've ever had to do in my life. She asked that I forgive Howard."

"She wh— Was she *insane*?! I mean, what in the holy hell?!" Willow blurted out.

"Yeah, I gotta say I'm with my mom on this one. That's pretty messed up," Sunny added.

Maisy snickered. "Trust me, I felt the same when she said it. I told her the chemo must have jumbled up her brain to make her say something that deranged. But in true Violet fashion she was thinking of my well-being. She knew the anger and hatred had consumed my life. She wanted me to be free of all of it. To let go of the bad and hold on to the good. Remember her and forget him. Let me tell you, I'll be damned if she wasn't right. It took me many years, but I was able to do it. And she wanted you two to forgive as well."

"Ooh, not sure I can do that, Maisy. You see, I'm a big believer in holding grudges and—"

"It won't happen overnight, Willow. Like I said, it took me *years*. But it was worth it. You must process it completely. Let it become a part of your soul and then simply let it go."

"Theora wouldn't happen to have a tea that could speed up that process, would she?" Willow asked with a smile.

After the three women hugged and said farewell, Willow and Sunny began driving down the mountain. Their lives had completely changed over the course of the last several hours and neither one had had a chance to stop and think about it. The car ride was the first time they'd been alone with their thoughts.

"You okay?" Sunny asked.

"Oh I'm just fan-fuckin-tastic. You?"

"I really don't know, mom. I mean, my God."

Willow let out a stifled laugh. "My entire life, literally all of it from conception until now, has been a total lie. I's laughin' at you for not realizing mama lived in a separate bedroom, and here I didn't know the first thing about her!"

"Honestly I just thought Maisy would be some old friend of mamaw's and she'd tell us that she didn't want the house and then things would be back to normal. I had no idea it would be so—" She cut herself off and mimed an explosion near her temple.

"Mama's the hero of the story and daddy's the villain. I did *not* see that coming," Willow said, shaking her head.

Sunny's mind was racing as she slowly drove down the winding road, but a thought suddenly occurred to her. "I'm going to write this story. This will be the legacy that I leave for Lilias. I finally know my family history. I mean, it's not a castle but it's a hell of a story for sure. Obviously, I won't give her every detail, but I think this could be really special for her some day." The truth was that she had already started coming up with short stories, fairy tales, and all sorts of life lessons from this newly discovered family narrative.

"That sounds like a good idea, Sunny girl. Be sure to send me a copy of it when you're done. A *signed* copy." Willow smiled and looked out the window of the car. Her smile slowly faded as she thought about Maisy. She couldn't begin to fathom how hard her life had been because of Howard. She wanted to make it right. She wanted to do something to help her.

Pulling into the driveway as the sun set, Willow looked at Sunny and asked, "Wait— So who owns the farmhouse?!"

Sunny's eyes grew wide before she closed them tight, laying her head against the steering wheel as she realized they completely failed to get an answer to the one question they set out to ask.

"Hey, Sun," Finley answered. She couldn't tell if his lowered voice indicated that he was still angry or if he was now apologetic.

"Hey, babe. How's Lil doing?"

"Oh she's alright. Been out in the garden with my maw all afternoon." He took a deep breath and said, "Look Sun, I feel terrible about how we left things. I was, as my granny would say, a complete eejit. I wasnae thinking straight. Lilias had just thrown a fit about God knows what and… I just hope you can forgive me. And I really do hope yer maw is okay. Were you able to find her?"

Sunny began smiling. "You have no idea how much I love you, Finley Graham. Yes, you can be an idiot sometimes, but the last forty-eight hours have been by far the most insane of my life. Hearing your voice is exactly what I need to feel grounded again. You are my normal."

"Well *that* was unexpected. I thought you were about to let me have it, and rightly so. Tell me what's happened, love," Finn said, relieved they were no longer fighting.

Sunny told him the whole story, from the safety deposit box to the fateful day in the barn between Howard and Violet. Retelling it not only helped Finn understand what all had transpired in Tennessee during her visit, but it helped solidify the story in her own mind so that she didn't forget any of the details.

"Christ, Sunny. I dinnae ken what to say. I'm sorry yer dealin' with this alone. And yer maw. How is she?"

"Honestly, I don't know. I mean, she seemed much better after the second trip. I can hear her moving around downstairs this morning, so at least she didn't run this time. God, so much of me wants to be in Scotland with you right now and away from all of this."

"Oh, there's a certain part of me that wants you to be here as well," Finn replied.

"Good Lord, Finn. Now's not the time! Get a hold of yourself," she said, giggling.

"Yeah, I'm gonnae have to, aren't I!" he shouted back.

"*Finn!*" Sunny was laughing harder than she had in days. When she finally caught her breath and was able to speak, she told him it was best she hung up and checked on her mother. "Who knows what adventures await us today? Personally, I'm hoping for a lazy day in pajamas. Give my love to Lil and tell her I'll call back tomorrow."

"I love you, Sunny. Dinnae ye ever forget that. And I'm proud of all yer doing there with yer maw." Finn knew he'd never fully trust or forgive Willow, but he could certainly empathize with her after hearing all that she was going through.

After hanging up, Sunny walked down the hall and looked at herself in the mirror above the bathroom sink. Somehow she thought she looked older, like all the information she'd learned over the last few days had aged her. She wondered if it was because she suddenly *felt* older. It was as if knowing all of the family secrets meant she was no longer a child. Sunny wondered if her mother felt the same way.

"Morning, mom!" Sunny said walking into the kitchen.

Willow was at the table drinking coffee and looking through the pages of an old *Farmers' Almanac*. "Mornin', Sunny girl. You sleep alright?"

"Surprisingly, yes. I thought for sure I'd have nightmares, but if I did I don't remember any of 'em. You?" Sunny poured herself a cup of coffee and joined her mother at the table.

"I got a few good hours."

"Well, what should we do today? Keep cleaning out the house or —"

"We're goin' back up to Maisy's," Willow said matter-of-factly.

"Aw shit," Sunny said as she laid her head down on the table. "You're joking, right?"

"Nope. I wanna bring her here so we can figure out this house situation once and for all." Willow stood up and rinsed her coffee cup out in the sink. "Finish your breakfast and we'll hit the road. And maybe change out of your pajamas, too." She walked out of the room leaving Sunny rattled and shaking her head.

"One day! I just want *one* lazy day!" Sunny shouted over her shoulder. Willow snickered as she made her way up the steps.

Back up the mountain they drove. Once Willow convinced Maisy to come to the farmhouse, they began driving back down the mountain. Maisy was unsure as to why she needed to visit the house, but Willow insisted. She knew the documents from the safety deposit box listed her as the rightful owner, but there was more to it than that. It had simply slipped her mind to bring it up during the previous day's conversations.

Sitting around the formal dining room table, Sunny organized the documents. The history of the house was on top and Violet's will was underneath.

Maisy politely looked through the papers and smiled. "Obviously I know about these, and I'm glad that you've both finally seen them. But this isn't Vi's final will."

"What do you mean?" Sunny asked.

"I have the final copy, as does their lawyer."

"Greenton?" Willow asked. "He never mentioned—"

"She told him not to. She didn't want Howard to know what was in her will. To be honest, all the things *in* the house weren't that important. The house itself was what she really cared about. Years ago, sometime in the early seventies, she drew up her will and put me down as the one who would get the house. She put a copy of that version in the safety deposit box and the other copy was with Mr. Greenton. Now once she got sick and things took a bad turn, she knew she was going to die before Howard. If he were to learn that I owned the house, well we just assumed he'd burn it to the ground out of spite. She couldn't bear leaving it to him, so she left it to the one person who meant the world to her." Maisy looked at Willow and smiled.

"You're kidding me," Willow responded.

Maisy laughed. "Not at all! You've owned the house ever since your mama died."

"Why didn't daddy know about her will? And if this isn't even his house, why did he add a clause in his will that I'm not allowed to sell the place?"

"Oh, this is where your mama really got the last laugh. Mr. Greenton had the most recent version of Violet's will, and I had the other copy. Vi told him that Howard wasn't to know about her will or the contents of it. So when Howard went in to have his will drawn up, thinking he owned the house and land, Mr. Greenton played it cool and Howard was none the wiser." Maisy was smiling while remembering Violet's antics. "And there never was a clause about you not selling the house. Howard's will actually said that the house and land should be turned over to the state or cleared for commercial use."

"*What?!*" Sunny and Willow shouted in unison.

"Exactly. Well, Mr. Greenton knew Howard didn't own the house, so anything he put in his will about the property was meaningless. But being the man he is he went along with it. Once Howard died, he wrote up some paperwork that *looked* like your father's will, but it was actually just something that assured the house was in your name with your signature on it. He made sure it was all legal so that nothing would come into question later on. I'm sure if you read through it all carefully you'll see what I'm talking about."

"Why would he do all of this? I mean, do all lawyers provide this level of personalized attention and get involved in family drama?" Sunny was suddenly very suspicious of the lawyer, if he was in fact a lawyer at all.

"Well, you all know him as Mr. William Greenton. Violet and I simply knew him as Billy." Maisy grinned.

"Billy?!" Willow exclaimed while smacking Sunny's arm.

Sunny's jaw dropped.

Maisy laughed. "That's it! Like I told you before, Billy and Violet went steady all throughout school and even during his first year at college. But they slowly drifted apart because of the long distance, and they each started making new acquaintances and dating others. I still believe that if he'd never left for school or if she'd gone with him, well, everything would have turned out differently. They always had fond memories of their times together. Even after Billy moved back here with his young bride, they never had sour feelings toward each other."

"But Mr. Greenton was such good friends with my daddy. Did he not know that he was mama's ex?" Willow asked.

"To everyone in town, Howard and Billy were good friends, but below the surface it was a different dynamic entirely. Howard knew that Billy and Violet had a history, and Howard was the kind of man that liked to keep his enemies close. Billy knew that Howard was nothing but trouble, so being friends with him seemed like the only way he could remain close with Violet and not cause suspicion. But anything Vi wanted, well Billy was more than happy to help her."

Willow looked confused and asked, "Then why would Mr. Greenton say that my daddy wanted me to keep the house? Why wouldn't he just tell me the truth so that I knew it was mama's all along?"

Maisy snickered. "And how would you have reacted to that? Would you have believed him?"

"Good point," Willow responded.

"Violet knew I would need to be the one to tell you the truth."

"Wow. I can't even— Just wow," Sunny said. "Okay so mom, you own the house. Right?"

"Yeah I guess I do, but I'm still not gonna live here. My life is in Knoxville. I can't move back now. There ain't nothin' for me here."

"So what are you going to do with it?" Sunny asked.

"Well, now that I know I own it I figure I'll ask good ol' Billy to help me draw up a will of my own and leave the house to you. Then you can leave it to Lilias when she's old enough. Hopefully she'll continue keepin' it in the family regardless of where we all live."

Sunny smiled. "It would make a beautiful vacation home for us to escape the city."

"As for now, Maisy, I'd love for you to live here. I mean, mama wanted this house to be yours way back when and it don't seem right that you had to live without her for all that time. Maybe living in the house you can feel close to her again."

Maisy chuckled. "Oh goodness. I'm not sure what to say. I can't leave Theora alone all the time. But I suppose I could spend the weekends in the mountains with her. Throughout the week she's busy with her patients, you know." Maisy started weighing the invisible pros and cons on her hands when she finally blurted out, "Oh to hell with it. Would you all help me move some of my flowers?"

Throughout the next two weeks, Sunny and Willow were busy cleaning out the remainder of Howard's belongings, all of which were donated to the local landfill. Maisy spent her time in the garden at her mountain shack picking out what to transplant to the farmhouse to rejuvenate the old garden. She wanted it to be as close to Violet's original garden as possible.

The day before Maisy was to officially move in, Willow and Sunny cleaned the house from top to bottom. In the rooms Sunny hadn't stress-cleaned earlier, years of dust and cobwebs were finally removed to reveal beautiful furniture and decorations that suddenly looked brand new again. The books in the study had visible titles and authors once more, and the windows allowed plentiful sunshine into the previously dim rooms. With their joints and muscles aching, Willow and Sunny sat down on the red velvet couch next to the upright piano. Sunny leaned her head against her mother's shoulder, exhausted but with a deep feeling of content.

"I'm so happy I came home this summer, mom."

"Oh, Sun. You have no idea how glad I am you're here. It's been... well, life changing," Willow said with a chuckle.

Sunny grinned. "I'm thinking I might still have time to get to Scotland for the last few weeks though. Would you be alright with that?"

"You don't need my permission. You're a grown woman! Get outta here and go see your husband and that sweet baby. Oh, and your new cow." She added the last part just to get a rise out of her.

"Ugh, I forgot about that goddamn cow. But seriously, will you be okay on your own? When are you going back to Knoxville?" Sunny was genuinely worried about Willow's state of mind. She was shocked there hadn't been another breakdown since the second trip.

"I'm alright, Sunny girl. I actually have a plan for when I get back."

Sunny sat up. "A *plan*?! Oh, do tell! This is very much unlike you Ms. Richmond."

"That right there. That's my first task. Sunny, I want to change my name to Willow Rose. I don't want the Richmond name anymore. It's been like a bad luck charm hangin' on my life since I's born and without it maybe I can finally have a fresh start."

"Jesus. That's a huge step, mom. I'm really proud of you." Sunny was taken aback, because her mother had never focused on self-healing.

"Thanks, Sun," she said with a smile. "Hell, who knows? I might even call up that shrink they had me seein' all them years ago. Or maybe I'll just go see Theora again." They both laughed.

"Oh man, Theora as a psychotherapist. Can you imagine?" Sunny asked, laughing harder.

Once they had settled down, Willow continued, "And another thing. I *am* going to come to New York to see you. You just let me know when it works for you and I'll be there. I don't care if I have to ride on a bus or fly in a plane, but I'm done bein' afraid of leavin' home. Lilias deserves better than what I been givin'. She needs a mamaw here in her own country to spoil her every once in a while and I can't do that if I'm not close to her."

"We'll pay for everything, mom. I promise. However you want to travel, we will pay for your ticket. My God, Lilias will lose her mind if she knows you're coming to New York."

They sat together on the couch for a while longer. Willow was running her fingers through Sunny's hair and thinking about all of her memories in the house. Knowing Maisy would be living there gave her a sense of peace. She couldn't imagine the house belonging to anyone else. Having a stranger's furniture in all the rooms and a stranger's knick-knacks on all the shelves became an emotional pain she couldn't bear to think about.

The hour was late and the women were about to go upstairs to bed, when Willow asked nervously, "Sunny, will you do me a favor?"

"Yeah, mom. What's up?"

Willow looked at the old piano. "Will you teach me how to play something?"

For the next hour Sunny taught Willow the only song she ever learned from Violet, and before the night was through Willow was able to play the first verse of Für Elise on the piano she had never been allowed to play. Watching her mother working so hard to hit the right keys, Sunny knew her recovery wouldn't be perfect. Willow was bound to make mistakes and get off key, but for the first time she could see how determined her mother was to get it right. It was a long overdue turning point in her life that they had both been craving.

The following morning, Sunny and Willow drove up the mountain in the old farm truck. At Maisy's shack, they loaded up all the plants she had picked out for the farmhouse garden and a small suitcase of clothing and toiletries. Theora was there to see her off and to say goodbye to Sunny and Willow.

"Oh I'm sure we'll see you again, Theo!" Willow said as she gave her a hug.

"I'm afraid not, little Willow. I've only a year or two left in this world. You must go and live your life. Our paths have crossed for the final time." Theora's smile was peaceful as Sunny gave her a hug as well. "I have something for the young Lily." She handed Sunny a necklace of dried heather.

Sunny held the necklace gingerly and said, "It's perfect, Theora. And thank you for everything."

They watched as Theora slowly walked back down the path to her home. Once she was out of sight they all climbed into the cab of the truck and made their way back down the mountain. At the farmhouse they unloaded the flowers and Maisy unpacked her things before they had lunch on the wrap-around porch.

"I can't count the number of meals I've had out here. Miss Cora used to serve us 'dandy tea' as she liked to call it, with raspberry jam on biscuits."

"Dandy tea? What's that?" Sunny asked.

"Dandelion tea! It was awful bitter, but Miss Cora would mix in so much honey that we didn't even notice. Sometimes we'd even smash some raspberries in it. That we'd call dandy juice!" Maisy was having a wonderful time recounting her childhood memories with Violet's daughter and granddaughter. She wished so much that Violet could be there with them. "I hope you girls know that you are welcome here anytime. Your bedrooms will always be there whenever you want to stay over. After all, this is your home!"

"I think we can just call it *our* home, Maisy. You're family now," Sunny said.

After lunch they walked through the house. Maisy told them all about the heirlooms they never knew anything about. The antique dishes in the dining room all had a story as to where they came from. Many of them were original to the house. In the pantry near the backdoor of the house, Maisy talked about how she and Violet would sneak out some nights to go stargazing after Cora had gone to sleep. They even found their initials carved into the underside of one of the shelves in the pantry.

Maisy pointed to one of the lower shelves and said, "And this, little Sunny, is where Violet would put out treats for you when you snuck down at night."

"She knew about that?! I thought I was being so sneaky!"

Maisy laughed. "She laid out treats to make it easier for you. Sometimes she'd catch you, but most of the time she'd let you get away. She thought it was the funniest thing to hear your little feet coming down those steps."

They moved through the various rooms until they reached the study. Maisy told them that the books belonged to Violet's great-grandmother, Cynthia, who had been a school teacher. Maisy walked around the desk and looked down to the corner.

"And the secret hideout. It was supposed to be a place to store a safe, but they never did install one. Willow, I know you have awful memories of it, but for Vi and me, well we had the best time with it as little girls. It was the perfect place to tell ghost stories or to pretend it was our own little home. In fact, Sunny I want you to check on something for me. Lean down there and open that up."

Sunny did as she was told and opened the secret nook.

"Now, underneath that little blanket one of those floorboards should be a little loose. See if you can't pry it up."

Sunny found the board she was talking about, but as a chronic nail-biter she wasn't able to pull it up without the aid of a letter-opener Willow handed her. Beneath the floorboard was a wrinkled envelope. Sunny picked it up and handed it to Maisy.

"It's still here! Oh, Violet. You really kept it all this time." Maisy put her hand to her mouth as she studied the envelope. She carefully pulled out a piece of paper that had been ripped apart and taped back together. "This was the first letter I sent her after she got married. The one Howard found. That loose floorboard was our *secret* secret hiding spot. She told me years ago that she had put the letter there, but I'm still shocked to see it again." Her eyes were filled with tears. Willow and Sunny could see that they were not from sadness but from knowing Violet loved her so deeply.

Sunny read the letter aloud:

Dearest Violet,

I hope this letter finds you well. I sincerely wish I could have been with you on your wedding day. I know you were a beautiful bride, even without a fancy wedding dress. I pray that you are safe and cared for. And I pray that your baby is born healthy and joyful.

It has been nearly two months with no word from you and my heart aches knowing this has become our new normal. Please understand that I am not angry with you, nor could I ever imagine a scenario in which I could feel anything other than love for you. My deepest fear has always been that you and I should be apart, and I see now that I am destined to live in this fear for the remainder of my days. My only hope is that we will find each other in whatever life awaits our souls beyond this world. Until then, I will never feel a happiness like I felt in your arms. My life will never feel as full as when I placed my grandmother's ring in your hand. And my heart will never love again.

Eternally yours,
Maisy

"Damn, Maisy. That was beautiful. I ain't never been given a love letter like that before. I don't care who it's from. Man or woman... that'd win me over for sure," Willow said, causing Maisy and Sunny to laugh.

"Oh we had so many adventures in this big old house. Everywhere I look there are more memories. It does my heart good to be here again," Maisy said with a look of pure happiness. Willow knew she made the right decision in asking Maisy to move in. Not only would she be able to keep an eye on things, but she belonged there. The home was a part of her life just as it was for all of them.

"I do have one more question for you, Maisy," Sunny said as they sat out on the porch that evening.

Maisy smiled. "Of course. Ask anything you'd like."

"Well, umm, where is she? My mamaw, where is she now?" Sunny realized as she asked it there was probably a better way to phrase the question.

Willow cocked her head to the side before blurting out, "What the hell, Sun?! She died, remember?"

"I know that, mom! Jesus! I just mean, you know, she's not buried with grampa, but we've cleaned this house from top to bottom and I never did find her ashes."

Maisy chuckled at their bickering. "We still have enough daylight left. Come walk with me." She got up from her chair and stepped off the porch. Sunny and Willow walked along the overgrown path with her. "I'll need to ask my nephew to mow these weeds down a bit so that I can get back here a little easier. You best watch out for snakes, and be sure to check for ticks tonight, okay?" Though she never had children of her own, Maisy was a natural caretaker. Sunny began to see her as a surrogate grandmother and couldn't wait to introduce her to Lilias one day.

As they walked down the small hill to the banks of the creek, Sunny and Willow watched as Maisy kicked off her shoes and continued walking straight into the steadily flowing stream. Turning her fingertips back and forth across the surface of the water with her eyes closed and a slight smile on her lips, she seemed to be transported to another time.

A few moments later she turned to look at them, still swaying in the current. "Violet asked that I place her ashes here in the creek, and to my surprise Howard didn't object. It was the one decent thing he ever did as far as I'm concerned. But this spot, oh this spot meant everything to us. It was our favorite place in the whole world from the time we were little girls until we were old, wrinkled women. And

I can still feel her here now. I know she's still here." As Maisy emerged from the creek, they notice a newfound air of serenity surrounding her, as if the water had washed away some of her grief. Knowing that Violet and Maisy were reunited through the creek brought both Willow and Sunny a great sense of happiness.

After spending one more night at the farmhouse, it was time to say goodbye. Maisy watched as Willow turned right to head toward her life in Knoxville, and Sunny turned left to head toward the airport in Charlotte, destined for New York and then Glasgow. The Rose farm had grown quiet once more, and Maisy began working in Violet's garden.

Weeks went by. Sunny spent them with Finley and Lilias in Scotland while Willow worked hard at starting her life over in Knoxville. After changing her last name to Rose, Willow began planning a trip to visit her granddaughter. She and Sunny talked to each other nearly every day. Sunny had started writing her grandmother's story so that it could be memorialized for future generations of their family. Violet's journey was hard, but the love she and Maisy shared was able to endure and that was a legacy to be proud of. At the end of summer, Sunny, Finn, and Lilias returned to New York and began preparing for kindergarten.

Maisy enjoyed her time at the farmhouse. The garden was looking much nicer since she'd cleaned out all the overgrown weeds and planted the new flowers. As planned, she would spend her weekends in the mountains with Theora. One Sunday afternoon as they were finishing their early supper before Maisy drove back to the farm, Theora decided to bring up something that had been plaguing her.

"I still don't understand how you did it," Theora said.

"Did what?" Maisy asked.

"Forgave him. Forgave that wicked man for all that he did."

"Oh why are you bringing that up now? That's all behind us. The girls are happy and they know the truth about him, so just let it go already." Maisy began clearing the dishes from the table.

"I'm a curious old lady. I like to know *how* things happen. That's why I stayed with Feng Chen, you know. This one time, he—"

"Not with the Feng Chen stories again! My God, anything but that." Maisy was shaking her head. She'd heard every Feng Chen story Theora had to offer multiple times. She knew all the punchlines, as well as every pause that had been added for dramatic effect. She began to feel like she'd actually met the man at some point in her life.

"If you don't want to hear about Feng, tell me how you forgave. I've known you since you were a child. Forgiveness is not your strongest attribute." Theora was giving her an accusing look.

"It's complicated, okay. Hell, I don't even know how I feel about it. But it's done. Violet wanted it done so I did it. Alright?" Maisy was getting flustered the more she spoke.

"You still haven't told me *how*," Theora said, grinning.

"You're not going to let this go, are you?" Maisy asked.

"Now that I know it gets under your skin... no. Besides, I am not good at forgiving either. I would like to know how." Theora took the last sip of her lemonade and handed the empty glass to Maisy.

"Oh don't be silly. What grudges are you holding?" Maisy asked with a scoff. She'd spent most of her life with Theora and had never heard her mention any kind of bad blood.

Theora said, "I have lived a very long life, a lot of which you are unaware of. And I only have a little time left to let things go. I would like to leave this world with peace in my heart."

Maisy rolled her eyes. "I don't know if my methods will work for you, Aunt Theora. I'm sorry."

"You think you know me so well. Why don't you just show me how you forgave him? It will be a simple trip because it all happened so recently. The mind will not have to search hard for the images."

Maisy stared out the window for a few moments. "Because I'm ashamed, Theora. I'm ashamed of how I handled it. I know what Violet wanted, but I took it a step too far. It was like I couldn't control myself, and I just—" She stopped herself before saying anymore.

"*Show me*," Theora pleaded.

After an internal debate with herself, Maisy reluctantly agreed. She watched as Theora mixed up a batch of reliving tea. They each added in a few drops of blood from their fingers and let the tea brew. Theora then ladled out a serving for Maisy into a Mason jar and closed the lid tightly. She poured out her own cup and they agreed to begin drinking at nine o'clock the following morning. Once Maisy returned to the farmhouse that evening, she tossed and turned all night debating whether or not it was a good idea. Ultimately, she decided to let Theora in and take her on the trip.

At nine o'clock sharp, both Maisy and Theora began drinking their tea. Maisy had walked down the path and sat upon the large stone in the middle of the creek, surrounded by the flowing water and the memories that built her life. Theora sat on a chair outside of her shack in the mountains. The sunlight, desperately trying to push through the foliage, was warm on their faces, but the air was crisp. Fall had arrived and the leaves were beginning their colorful transition before returning to the earth. Once the teacups were empty, they closed their eyes as Maisy began her meditation.

*The sweet scent of bluebells. . . . . hot soup on a cold night. . . . .
a slow song on the piano. . . . . hands clasped together in the
dark. . . . . a whisper and a smile. . . . .*

The headlines scrolling across the television announce that
Saddam Hussein has been sentenced to death by an Iraqi tribunal. It
is early November 2006, and Violet has been gone for well over a
year. Howard is sitting in the living room nearly asleep in his recliner.
There is a knock at the front door that startles him. He opens the door
to find Maisy with a bouquet of flowers, her head slightly bowed.
Howard looks puzzled as he clears his throat, uncertain it's truly her
standing before him.

"The hell are you doin' here?" he asks.

"I've come to forgive you, Howard, and I hope you can forgive
me as well." Maisy is struggling to get the words out, as it goes
against everything she feels.

Howard is speechless for a moment. "Now why would I wanna
do that? And why would you, for that matter?"

"Oh believe me, it was Violet's idea. I brought these flowers for
you as a symbol of forgiveness and humility. I hope that you will
accept them."

Howard looks at them. "What kind are they?" he asks.

"Bluebells. Violet really liked them." Maisy feels as if she is
betraying Violet by speaking with him so freely, but she also knows it
is what she wanted. She hands Howard the flowers and quickly adds,
"Just put them in a vase with some water. They should last a week or
so as long as they get a little sunlight throughout the day."

Howard takes the flowers and says, "Uh, yeah, thanks. You, uh,
have a nice day now." He closes the door as Maisy walks off the
porch toward her car. Behind the closed door he puts his nose to the
flowers and inhales. Their sweet scent fills his mind with memories
of Violet, and for a moment he mourns her.

Months pass and in the middle of winter Howard receives another knock at the door. He answers and is happy to see Maisy has returned, though he dares not show it. Since Violet's passing he has become quite lonely, and the bitter cold winter months only worsen his feelings of isolation. This time she does not carry flowers with her but is instead holding a crock of warm soup.

"You bring some sort of forgiveness stew?" he asks. His tone is harsh, but that is not his intention.

"It's awful cold out here, Howard. The polite thing would be to invite me in for a moment," Maisy replies. She speaks with the confidence of a woman who does not tolerate a pompous man.

Howard steps back and allows her to enter the farmhouse. She proceeds to the kitchen, making herself at home. She pulls out two bowls, two spoons, and two napkins. Howard walks in to see her setting the small table. He scratches his head.

"Howard, you don't look like you've had a real meal all winter, so sit down and eat. I made a big pot of potato soup last night and I figured you might like some." Maisy is trying her hardest to be polite per Violet's wishes, but it is proving harder than she ever imagined.

He sits at the table, unsure about the entire situation. Maisy fills his bowl with soup and then her own. "What would you like to drink?" she asks before taking her seat. He asks for sweet tea and she pours two glasses. She sits across from him and begins eating her soup. Still confused, Howard begins eating and is surprised at how good it tastes. Maisy can tell he is enjoying it, and she is pleased.

They finish eating, and she cleans up the table. Howard walks her to the door and thanks her for the soup. She asks if he would like her to bring food more regularly, and he hesitantly answers that he might enjoy that. She nods and walks to her car as he closes the door.

For the next two years, Maisy brings Howard a meal at least once a month. There are times where she visits once a week with food for him. Their conversations become longer and longer. Howard looks forward to her visits, not only for the food but for the company as well. He no longer feels the loneliness that was brought on by Violet's passing, and for that he is grateful. He particularly enjoys when Maisy plays the piano. It has been so many years since Violet's songs filled the house, and he realizes how much he misses the slow melodies.

It is early spring and Maisy sits on the porch next to Howard. They are looking out at the overgrown fields and eating homemade banana bread. The birds are singing loudly as the first signs of green leaves begin to peek out from the tree branches.

"This farm has always been so peaceful," Maisy says. "I've loved it since I was a child. You know, I might have more memories of this home than of my own. Isn't that something?"

Howard nods. "Yeah, that's somethin' alright. It's quite the house, I'll give you that. I never could make much out of the land though. Your daddy and Archie, they was the real farmers 'round here. Perhaps after I die someone else can make use of it."

Maisy raises an eyebrow and asks, "Well, won't it belong to Willow at that point?"

"Nah," Howard waves her question off. "She ain't gonna get this place. She'd probably just turn it into a whorehouse or a meth lab."

"*Howard!*" she scolds. "That is not how you should be talking about your daughter. She's had rough times, but it seems like she's doing alright now. She's holding down a job in Knoxville, right? If Violet taught me anything it's that forgiveness *is* possible." She looks at him over the rim of her glasses.

"Oh I ain't mad at her, Maisy. I just think she's better off without this house. Seems like she's had nothin' but bad memories in this town so no use in tethering her to it with this place."

"So you're going to sell it?" she asks.

Howard shakes his head. "No, ma'am. I had my will updated so that the state can take this place. I don't care if it turns into a damn shoppin' mall."

Maisy frowns but says nothing more about it.

The following week they talk about the weather and how they each think the new president is doing. At the next week's visit, Howard is not feeling well. Maisy does not stay long in order to keep herself healthy, but she brings him some chicken noodle soup to help him feel better. Over the next four weeks, Howard's health does not improve. He has not seen a doctor as he swears it's "just a little bug". Maisy urges him to make an appointment, but he once again refuses.

"Howard, you've been coughing for weeks! You're struggling to breathe at times! I think you might have pneumonia, and you need to see a doctor before it gets worse." Maisy warns, but Howard ignores her.

"Bah! Willow's comin' home next weekend. She's houndin' me about seein' a doctor as well. I'll let her take me when she's back," Howard says, finally conceding.

Maisy arrives the following Friday in the early part of the evening. Howard answers the door and he is feeling much better.

"See? No doctor needed. I told you it was just a bug," Howard says as she walks in.

She carries in a pot of corn chowder and smiles at him. He is happy to see her and eager to eat a large meal after a month-long illness. Howard sets the table while Maisy puts the soup on the stove. While waiting for their meal to heat up, they make their way into the living room. Maisy sits on the couch, expecting Howard to sit in his recliner. Instead he sits next to her, and her heart beats faster.

"This okay?" he asks. "You know, me sittin' here?"

She smiles. "Of course. Of course it's okay."

They talk a while longer until Maisy says the soup is likely ready. They sit at the table together, eating and sharing a lively conversation. After cleaning up the dishes they decide to sit on the porch to watch the sunset. The storm clouds from earlier in the day are creating a breathtaking view along the horizon. Howard places his hand on Maisy's. Her muscles become tense, her heart pounds.

After the sun disappears, Howard suggests they go back in the house. "I'm not sure I'm completely over that bug, Maisy. I'm feelin' awful wore out."

"Yes, let's get you inside, Howard. You should really lie down."

Maisy helps him to his feet and walks him into the house. He points to the staircase and together they make their way to the master bedroom where he seems to stand up a little taller and not need as much support.

"Ain't that the damndest thing? I'm not a hundred percent yet, but I don't feel nearly as bad as I did on the porch." He begins unbuttoning his shirt and asks, "It feel hot in here to you?"

"No, I think it feels alright. Maybe you ought to just go to bed, Howard. I bet you need a good night's sleep to shake whatever this is. I think you've just done too much too soon." Maisy stands near the door as she watches him undressing, her heart beating faster.

"Yeah. Maybe I should just rest a little," he says. He takes off his shirt and pants and lies on the bed. Maisy picks up his clothes and places them in the hamper before walking back toward the door. He stops her by asking, "Oh, Maisy. Won't you stay a little longer with me?"

She smiles and nods her head. "Of course, Howard." She moves a chair to the edge of the bed and sits down next to him. Their eyes meet and she smiles at him. Beads of sweat form on his forehead, and he begins to shiver. His breath becomes a struggle as he reaches for her hand. She holds it tightly and asks, "What is it Howard? What's wrong?"

"*Help me, Maisy! Please, help me! I... I can't—*" he begs, gasping for air.

As the poison from the hemlock continues spreading throughout his now paralyzed body, Howard's eyes fill with terror as Maisy leans down next to his ear and whispers, "*BE STILL!*"

Sitting on the stone in the middle of the creek, Maisy smiled through her meditative state as Theora's laughter echoed down the mountain.